GHOSTS ARE ASSHOLES

JAMES KIRST

World Castle Publishing, LLC
Pensacola, Florida
Copyright © James Kirst 2018
Paperback ISBN: 9781949812152
eBook ISBN: 9781949812169
First Edition World Castle Publishing, LLC, November 12, 2018
http://www.worldcastlepublishing.com

Licensing Notes
Cover: Karen Fuller
Editor: Maxine Bringenberg

CHAPTER 1

Ghosts are assholes. They always demand things. Give this ring to my fiancée. Give this teddy bear to my daughter. Find out who murdered me. Find out how I died. And so on and so forth. And are they ever grateful? No, of course not. They never even say thank you.

"Why? Why? Why?" I heard her cries late into the night. Why, why, why? At first I tried ignoring her. Didn't work. I threw one of my pillows at her to try and shut her up. It worked as well as you might expect. She just stared at me as my eyes were drawn to that bloody gash on the top of her head that seemed to stream blood down to her eyes, and made it appear as if she were crying blood.

I furiously sat up from where I lay. "Would you please, please shut up?" I screamed, glaring at her.

The pale white girl with red splotches that decorated her torso and legs in an almost random fashion just ignored me and continued her repetitious cries of "Why?" I groaned as I slammed my head against my

5

other pillow and quickly covered my head with it in a vain attempt to drown her out. I was upset, but honestly, it was something I should have been used to by then. These kinds of things had been happening since the first ghost I met.

The first thing you need to know about ghosts is that not everyone can see them. Only those of a certain bloodline or lineage are able to do so, and even then, whether you have the gift or not is really up to chance.

I remember when I saw my first ghost—I couldn't have been more than eight or nine years old at the time. I woke in the early morning hours for no particular reason. You know how it is; you wake up for a moment, maybe move over to the side a little bit, adjust yourself, and immediately fall back asleep. Except this time, I noticed a pale figure with a pale white mustache, combed over hair, wearing a vest over a T-shirt and what appeared to be dress pants, sitting on the foot of my bed staring at me.

At first, I thought it was a strange dream—I mean, I could literally see through the man. But after pinching myself a couple of times, as they did in all the cartoons, I quickly realized I wasn't asleep.

I didn't dare move a muscle. I was almost literally frozen with fear. I wound up not getting any more sleep that night, and when my mother entered my room to wake me up for school, she was surprised to see me awake. "Vincent, you're certainly up early!"

I whispered back, "Mom, there's somebody on my bed."

Initially, she just smiled at me. "Really, Vincent? Well, who could that be?" Her smile slowly faded, and her voice trailed when she turned her head and saw the apparition. "Vincent, you can see him?" she asked. I nodded my head silently in confirmation. "That's amazing! I cannot believe it—you have the gift!"

I didn't know this before that night, but apparently my mother has been able to see ghosts her entire life. I suppose it should have been obvious; my mother was and is a spirit medium, after all. I had assumed, though, that my mother wasn't really communicating with the dead. I didn't think she was outright scamming people, mind you. I just thought it was like fortune telling, where people generally know it's fake but they still pay for it for entertainment purposes. Little did I know that ghosts were real.

It was well believed that only the females of our family were able to see ghosts, hence my mother's surprise. Indeed, I was the first male ever with this "gift," as my mother calls it. I don't quite agree with her that it's a gift, but I suppose it's a matter of perspective. She believes I have this ability because I'm such a sensitive young man, which really raises my self-esteem quite a bit.

My mother claims that we are descendants of the Biblical Witch of Endor. She was the witch who summoned Samuel back from the dead at the command of Israel's

7

King Saul, at least according to legend. Personally, I'm not sure if I believe the tale, and I certainly don't believe that our genealogy can be traced to the Witch of Endor. It's probably like the Mayflower; everyone from Boston claims to be a descendent of one of the immigrants that arrived on that ship, but very few actually are. Now that I think about it, did the witch even have any children?

"Why? Why? Why?" My ghostly invader continued to whine throughout the night.

"Look, I don't know why," I growled, sitting up once again. "And right now I don't care. It's late. I'm tired. I've had a long day. If you would just shut up until morning, I might be able to help you out and maybe figure out 'why,' and maybe 'who,' 'what,' 'where,' and 'when' as well. Maybe 'how,' too, if I'm feeling especially generous. Are we clear?"

"Why? Why? Why?" she ignored me and continued to incessantly whine.

I let out a loud groan and let my head hit the pillow again. "Why me?" I whined to the ceiling. "Why does this keep happening to me?"

The second thing to remember is that I don't see every ghost out there in the world. In fact, I usually only see one ghost at a time. Ghosts basically just randomly appear before me. I kind of assume there are hundreds if not thousands or millions or billions of ghosts roaming this planet that are invisible to me, which is unfortunate because if I can't see them, probably nobody else in this city can see them either. These poor souls are just wandering around, wailing about their fate. At least, that's what I assume. To tell the truth, I'm not actually sure what they are doing. I also have no idea why I'm able to see some and not others, and what allows them to be visible and able to communicate with the living.

My mother has some theories. She believes that the reason why ghosts remain hidden most of the time is because the vast majority of people cannot see or hear them no matter what they try. They tend to assume that this is true of everyone as a result. Since most people don't believe in ghosts, it appears that most ghosts don't believe in mediums. This obviously makes communication very difficult.

Her theory is supported with her work. She tells clients that she doesn't guarantee she'll be able to contact the dead, and that she is at most a conduit that provides ghosts the ability to speak to the world of the living. Basically, during a séance, she sends out a message telling ghosts "I'm available" and "I'm listening." Doing that seems to increase the odds that a ghost will appear and talk to her. I don't usually make a great effort to talk to ghosts, so I talk to them far less than my mother does. It's as good a theory as any, I suppose.

Of course, the capricious nature of ghosts can make life quite difficult for a medium. I remember my senior year. I was on the football team. My primary motivation at first for playing was to prove to everyone that I wasn't a sensitive little boy. But over time, I grew to love the sport.

It happened during the big homecoming game. We were playing against our rivals and we just needed a touchdown to win the game. During the last play of the game, I was able to break free and was wide open as I ran towards the end zone. The ball was heaved in my direction and I was about to make the game winning catch.

"Hey buddy! You gotta help me!" A large young man suddenly appeared before me. In response, I reflexively closed my eyes, slowed my pace, put my shoulder down, and braced for impact, only to find absolutely no resistance. The jarring effect between expectation and reality made me trip over my own feet, and I fell down face first in the grass as the ball sailed over me and fell harmlessly to the ground. It was then I realized that the man who appeared before me was actually a ghost.

Like I said, it's almost random when a ghost is able to appear before someone like me, and a muscular ghost, with what was probably blond hair and that wore a letterman's jacket over a football jersey and blue jeans, just happened to appear at the biggest moment of my life to that point. It wasn't his fault, I recognized that. Still, this didn't prevent me from being enraged with the ghost, as unfair as that might have been.

I mean, think about it. Nobody else saw the ghost, so it just looked like I tripped at the most crucial moment of the game. This hardly helped my reputation at school, and for quite a while I had to deal with the ire of my classmates. The whispers I heard behind my back, the mockery in the school paper, the fact that my date for homecoming suddenly came down with the "flu," — they made things very miserable for me for a little while, and I took my frustration out on my ghostly acquaintance. It was about a week before I finally began speaking to the apparition in a civilized manner.

"Okay, look, let me put it this way," I said to the young female spirit, rising again from where I lay, feeling enraged at this point. "If you don't quit asking me why, I'm going to take that revolver in my desk, place it to my temple, and blow my brains out, and I will guarantee that I will haunt this place with you, and every time you ask me 'why?' I'm going to answer, 'Because you wouldn't shut up!' So again, I ask you, I beg of you—please, let me sleep."

Her moans abruptly stopped. After what seemed to be a long period of silence, I heard a meek, demure voice say, "Okay."

"Okay as in, 'I'm going to let him sleep all night and not say anything until the morning,' or okay as in 'I'm going to say okay but as soon as his guard's down, I'm going to continue whining'? Because I know how you ghosts operate, and I know you guys tend to do that."

"The first one."

"Good. Thank you." With that, I was able to rest my

11

head against my pillow and fall asleep almost instantly.

The third thing you need to know about ghosts, as I alluded to earlier, is that they always want something. Often it is one last task that they weren't able to complete. That's how it was for the ghosts I talked about earlier. The name of the first ghost, the ghost who had kept me up all night by staring at me, was William Hunter. A divorced father of one, he was on his way to visit his son to take him home for the weekend. There, he would give him a gift he knew his son would love, an official NBA basketball. His plan was to play with him at the park over the weekend.

Unfortunately, a drunk driver had put an end to those plans in a head-on collision on the highway. Both he and the driver were killed immediately. He wanted to give his son that basketball to let him know that his father was thinking of him just before the end. It was my mother's job to do this final task for him.

Of course, my mother had to explain to the man that finding that specific basketball would have been nearly impossible. Either the police already had it in their evidence locker or, more likely, it was simply destroyed in the crash.

William settled for my mother buying another basketball and giving it to his son anonymously. It couldn't just be any basketball, though—it had to be an official NBA basketball, so my mom had to go to a sporting goods store and buy the most expensive ball in the shop. You better believe I brought this up, and was quite upset when I received a generic basketball for my birthday. Women's size.

With the help of William, we were able to find his ex-wife's home. To this day I can still see my mother from the passenger's side of that car, knocking on the door and dashing back to the vehicle moments before the confused son opened the door. Bewildered, the son looked around a bit before noticing the package on the ground.

His eyes opened wide and he smiled when he saw the basketball. He lifted it to his face and noticed the label. His joy quickly turned to sadness. The label read, "To: Jeremy, Love Always: Dad." My last image of William was him fading away as he attempted in vain to hug his son, who was in his mother's arms crying and calling out for his dad.

Yet did William ever thank my mother for any of her efforts? Of course he didn't. I know he had other things on his mind, but a small little thank you before he left would have been nice. My mother didn't mind; she tends to forgive things like that. I don't. A little gratitude goes a long way.

Another ghost who wanted something was Warren—the guy who interrupted my game winning catch. He'd played on my high school's football team way back in the day. His team actually won his homecoming game, an irony that was not lost on me. Before he could take his lovely date Suzy Charles to the dance, however, he celebrated his victory with some friends and basically drank himself to death.

He wanted me to tell Suzy how much she meant to him and how much he loved her. To do that, he asked me to give her his high school ring. He had planned to give it to her during his homecoming dance as an expression of his love. Since he did not make it to the dance, for obvious reasons, and could no longer give the ring to her in his present state, it was up to me.

A horrific thought crossed my mind, initially. I told Warren that if he was buried with that ring he would have to find someone else to help him out. I may be a lot of things, but I certainly didn't want to be a grave robber. Warren assured me that he was sure he wasn't wearing his class ring at the time of this death. He actually never wore it; he'd bought it strictly to give to Suzy. Trusting a ghost is always a recipe for disaster, but this time, the revulsion I had towards exhuming his body made me surprisingly amenable towards believing my ghostly acquaintance.

Thus, I had decided that the first course of action was to see whether his family was still in this city, and whether any of them had the ring. Through conversations with Warren, various Internet searches, and perusal of social media sites, I was able to find out some rudimentary information on Warren's family.

His parents had died recently. Neither parent was ever in particularly great health, so their lifestyle had finally taken its toll. The father had died only a few months before I met Warren, apparently from lung cancer, and his mother had died from a heart attack only a month prior to my meeting with the ghostly football player.

The only other family member Warren had was his sister, Anna. Luckily for me, Anna was still around, relatively speaking at least. Though she had moved out of this city, she still lived in state, which was pretty fortunate all things considered. Granted, she lived in Marysville, which was about an hour and a half drive from where I lived in Tacoma. But still, she lived near enough that if she had the ring I could get it easily.

I contacted Anna through a social media website. Modern technology makes contacting people surprisingly easy, especially since Anna had made her profile public.

Now, actually asking whether she had the ring and whether she could part with it, and even why I was talking to her in the first place, was challenging. It's not as if you can say, "Your brother's ghost is talking to me, and needs to give this ring to a girl he dated in high school in order to rest in peace." She would have never answered me, and I would have been blocked immediately.

Instead, I told her that my father had died recently and was from the same class as her brother. His class ring was a prized possession of his, and I had, unfortunately, lost it. Still, I thought it would be appropriate for him to be buried with a class ring from the year he graduated, even though it wasn't technically his own, if only for the symbolism. I also told her that she was the fifth person I had asked about the ring, the previous four either refusing to part with the ring or not having one to give.

That's one of the things about seeing ghosts and helping ghosts that you must realize—you have to become very adept at lying. Very few people actually believe in ghosts, and those that do probably aren't the kind of people you would want to meet, so it's often better to come up with a plausible falsehood than to tell the truth.

Fate, in many ways, was definitely on my side. His sister had the ring. Her parents had kept all Warren's possessions, having been unable to part with them after his death. After Warren's mother passed on, his things were inherited by his sister.

It's worth pointing out that through my discussions with Warren, I got the impression that he and his sister weren't the closest of siblings, an idea that was cemented during my conversation with her. She told me that she, as she put it, was stuck with his crap after her mother died. When I asked whether she would be willing to give me the ring, she told me that she couldn't ever think about parting with her brother's most prized possession...for free.

After doing some haggling the two of us were finally able to come to a price we both could agree on, though I do think she took advantage of the fact that I was a "grieving son looking for something to bury his father with." Let me just say the price was a little more than I could afford on my own, and I had to borrow some of the sum from my mother. She understood, though, as she had experienced similar problems with her misadventures with ghosts.

A long drive to Marysville later, I was in possession of the ring. The sister barely said anything to me before practically snatching the money out of my hand. After a quick count to make sure all of it was in the envelope I gave her, she shoved the ring into my hand and slammed the door behind her. I might have said an expletive or two afterwards and made a rude gesture or three behind her back in response. Still, all her faults aside, she wasn't a swindler, as I immediately checked and confirmed that the ring was exactly the one I needed.

The next step was to actually give the ring to Suzy. Finding Suzy was also a bit of a task, though not a Herculean one, admittedly. Once again, social media websites greatly simplified what could have been an arduous process. At first, I could not find her anywhere; I mean, I could find hundreds of women named Suzy Charles, but I could not find Warren's Suzy Charles. During my searches, though, I had an epiphany, and realized that she probably no longer went by the name Suzy Charles, and had probably married in the time between high school and the current day.

I then asked Warren if he could remember some of

17

his friends from his class, and luckily for me he was a relatively popular guy and could list a multitude of friends. Through these friends I was able to search through various posts, pictures, friends' lists, and other like items on the social media site to eventually find the woman we were looking for.

She now went by the name Suzy Brown, having married a man named Thomas Brown, a man who had not gone to Warren's high school, nor was he even from the state. Through his business dealings he had befriended a few of Warren's old high school buddies, and it was through them that he'd met Suzy. It was through their pages that I was able to find out all of this information.

It took Warren a minute to recognize the woman. She had aged thirty years since high school, of course, but he eventually did recognize her and confirmed she was the one we wanted to find. Locating her wasn't very difficult at this point, either. Her address wasn't displayed on any of her social media pages, but a quick yellow page search allowed me to locate her relatively easily. With that information in tow I was able to find out where Suzy lived, and was on my way to deliver the ring to her.

I felt like a detective, though granted, the task was immensely easy seeing that virtually none of her information was hidden and most of it was public. Let that be a lesson to you; if you are on a social media site, always make your information private.

Anyway, the married couple now lived in Lacey,

which was only about a half hour drive south of Tacoma. A bit of a drive, but not nearly as daunting as the one to Marysville.

Now, the plan was for me to drive over to Suzy's house, place the ring on her doorstep, and run to the car just before anyone caught me. Warren was worried that he wouldn't get to see Suzy, but I had assured him that he would see her when she answered the door. He also asked what would happen if Suzy wasn't home, so I assured him that he could wait there and eventually she would get home, and eventually she would get the ring. I also told him that I'd wait in the car from across the street just in case, and wouldn't leave until I confirmed she got the ring. The ghost eventually agreed to this scheme, and said it was a good one.

We arrived at the woman's house. As I walked up to the door, I instructed Warren to stand right at the doorway while I executed my plan. He nodded in confirmation and stood silently while I nodded back. I reached my hand back to knock. My hand was just about to hit the large, wooden door when suddenly a middle-aged woman wearing a pink blouse and black pants, her brunette hair in a bob, appeared in front of me. I nearly punched the woman in the face, but luckily I was able to hold my fist back just in time.

"Oh my God! I am so sorry!" I exclaimed.

"Oh no," she said, after taking a few seconds to regain her composure. "It was my fault. I just happened to be looking out the window when I saw you park in the driveway. I thought I'd open the door and greet you before you had a chance to knock, but I apparently didn't get here fast enough." She then chuckled lightly. "So tell me, what are you selling, mister?"

"Pietro, Vincent Pietro," I answered. "And I'm not really here to sell anything."

"What's that on the ground?" she asked, her attention now transfixed on the ring box that was sitting by my feet. Before I could answer, she reached down and picked up the box. "Oh, it's a ring. Is this yours?"

"Not exactly," I replied, trying to fumble through what I should say to the poor woman. This certainly wasn't part of the plan.

She pulled the ring out of the box and examined it carefully. Normally I would have mentioned that it was rude to examine a stranger's ring, but unfortunately my mind was preoccupied trying to think of a reason for exactly why I was there. "Oh my God, it's a ring from my senior high school class. What are you doing with this ring, young man?"

"Honey, is everything all right?" I could hear a man's voice from within the house.

"Yes, everything is fine, dear," the woman said. A tall man in horn rimmed glasses, wearing a plaid suit and bowtie, pipe in mouth, clean shaven, and hair cut short, appeared next to Suzy at the doorway. "Thomas," she continued, "This young man has a class ring from

20

my senior year in high school."

"Interesting. Why do you have a ring from her high school class, young man?" It was then that Warren thought it would be a great idea to start blathering on to Suzy that he loved her and that he would always love her and begging her to see him. Of course, I had explained to Warren a countless number of times that my mother and I were the only ones who could see him, but apparently when he actually saw the love of his life he forgot about all of that and couldn't resist blabbing on and on.

"Um," I said, trying desperately hard to ignore Warren, "Did you know a Warren Ericson?"

"Warren Ericson?" Suzy asked. "Now where did I hear that name before?"

"Suzy, you remember me, right? Your darling Warren!" Warren screamed this in my ear, annoying me greatly.

"I believe he was a friend of yours in high school," I said, still trying to ignore his screams.

"Perhaps you are right," she said, looking up in the air thinking. "Oh!" she exclaimed suddenly. "I know who you are talking about. Poor Warren Ericson. The poor fool drank himself to death, didn't he?"

"I knew you remembered me!" exclaimed Warren, "I love you so much, Suzy!"

"He wanted you to know that he always loved you," I said, my head getting sore by this point.

"Oh, he did?" Suzy said in response, "Oh, that poor,

poor boy."

"Excuse me for being nosy," Thomas said, pulling the pipe out of his mouth. "But how do you know all of this?"

"Yes, that is an excellent question," Suzy said.

"I'm so sorry, Suzy. We should have been together. We were meant to be together!" Warren screamed.

For a few moments, I couldn't think of anything to say. Various fibs and lies were flooding my brain, but I couldn't think of anything solid or believable to say. It didn't help my thinking process that Warren continued to obliviously rant in my ear about how much he loved Suzy, and it also did not help that Thomas and Suzy were constantly peppering me with questions, such as asking me how I knew all of this and what exactly I was doing there. My head began to pound. A cold sweat began to form on my back and the back of my neck. Anxiety overcame me. I began rubbing my neck as I tried to decide exactly what I should say.

"Look!" I blurted out suddenly. "Are either of you religious or spiritual in any way?"

"Oh, are you a missionary?" Suzy asked.

"He certainly isn't dressed like a missionary," Thomas said.

"No, I'm not a missionary!" I shouted. "I just wanted to know if either of you are religious."

"Well," Thomas said, "I don't know if we are particularly devout. We do go to church every now and again, and I do believe there may be something out there greater than us. But then again, maybe not. Why do you ask?"

"Okay, so you at least understand that there are all sorts of people in the world with all sorts of beliefs," I said in response.

"Of course," Thomas said.

"Yes, absolutely," confirmed Suzy.

"I know both of you will probably think I'm crazy, but what if I told you that Warren told me this?" The husband reached for the door and the couple took a step or two backwards. "I meant through a journal! Through a journal!" The couple inched forward and continued to listen.

"My mom and Warren's sister Anna are really good friends. We were helping her move when I tripped over a box and found Warren's journal, as well as the ring. I read the journal. Nosy, I know. Not proud of it, but it is what I did. The journal talked about how much he loved you and wanted the two of you to be together, and that he wanted to give you this ring at your homecoming dance, that sort of thing. Because of this, I thought it'd be appropriate for you to have the ring, so I looked up your information online." Like I said, you need to be adept at lying in my line of work, though Warren seemed to disagree, screaming in my ear asking why I was lying. I ignored him as best I could.

"Online?" Thomas asked.

23

"Yeah, through social media and the yellow pages, that sort of thing," I confirmed.

"Suzy, I told you we shouldn't share all that information online," her husband scolded.

"We'll talk about that later," Suzy snapped back. "So you think he wanted me to have this ring, then?"

"Yes, I absolutely do."

"I can't accept this."

"Please," I begged. "I believe that a person's soul cannot rest in peace until his final task is completed. I would feel much better if you simply took the ring. It's what he would have wanted."

"May I see the journal?" Suzy asked.

"I forgot it at home," I said, obviously having nothing to give her. "Please, you have to trust me on this one. Please just take the ring."

"Just do it, honey," Thomas said in a weary tone.

"Okay," Suzy said sheepishly. "Thank you very much. Good luck with your life, young man."

"Yes, thank you," her husband responded gruffly. "Now please leave, sir, before I am forced to call the cops."

"Okay, I'm going. Sheesh," I said in response.

Warren remained at the steps as I began walking towards the car. "She took it!" I heard Warren say wistfully. "She took the ring! I will always love you, Suzy! Remember me!" Warren's voice began to diminish, and I looked over my shoulder to see that he was fading into the ether. He was gone by the time I heard the door slam shut.

Warren didn't thank me either. I don't ask for much, a little show of appreciation is all I really want. Even a simple, "Good job" would suffice. But no, a ghost is never thankful for anything.

Like I said earlier, a lot of times ghosts want you to complete their final task, but that's not always why a ghost sticks around on earth. Almost equally as often a ghost simply wants to know how he or she met their grisly demise. Now, add clairvoyance to my list of supernatural powers if you would like, because somehow I knew that my intruder would want to know why she died. It was just a hunch.

CHAPTER 2

"Hey you! Good morning!" The ghost girl's face hovering just above mine was apparently going to be my alarm clock that morning.

"For the love of God!" I screamed, falling quite literally out of bed. "Don't do that!" I bellowed, rising to my knees. "You scared the hell out of me!"

"Sorry! I didn't mean to scare you! I just wanted to wake you up."

"What time is it, anyway?" I asked, throwing the blanket off me.

"I don't know. I just got bored and wanted to wake you up."

I took a look at my clock. "Seven-thirty," I said. "You only gave me about five hours of sleep."

"I tried to wake you up earlier," she explained as I rose from the floor, "When the sun rose. But you muttered a very harsh two-word answer in return. I thought it'd best just to let you sleep."

26

"I wish you had let me sleep a little longer," I said, stretching at the side of my bed, "Oh well. Not a big deal, I suppose. Just don't scare me next time, all right?"

"Are you going to find out how I died today, then?" she asked.

"Yeah, eventually," I replied. "I want to eat some breakfast first and take a shower, not to mention I need to use the bathroom. Speaking of which," I said, putting my index finger out towards the ghost girl, "Would you excuse me for a second?" I then lumbered over to my tiny, dirty bathroom a short distance from my bed.

"Close the door behind you, at least," she said in response, turning her head and body away from me.

"Sorry, used to being alone in this house," I said.

"Well?" she inquired.

"Well what?"

"Aren't you going to close the door?"

"I'll be done in a second. Besides, you're a ghost, right? It's not like a door would stop you."

"It doesn't mean I want to see you peeing," she said as I flushed the toilet. "Are you done?"

"Yes, but—"

She turned before I could complete the sentence, and then immediately turned around again. "Oh my God, you're naked!" she said sheepishly.

"Like I said, I wanted to take a shower. Are you sure you don't want to watch?"

"Oh, God no."

27

"Your loss," I said, as I entered the shower. I decided to take an extra-long one, and I was sure to sing as loudly and obnoxiously as possible. I don't even remember if I had ever sung in the shower before that day. After finishing and drying myself off, I said to the ghost girl, "I'm wearing a towel now, if you want to take a look at me again."

"I'll wait until you are completely dressed, thank you," she said in response.

"I'm not that bad looking, am I?" I asked, as I fished around in my closet for my favorite khaki pants and button up shirt. "I've been working out lately."

"It's not that, you look fine. It's just I don't even know your name. We just met."

Still just wearing a towel, I combed my brown hair and said to my ghostly acquaintance, "Fair enough. I'm Vincent Pietro. Now that you know my name, you're fine with seeing me naked, right?"

"That's not what I meant at all!" she shouted, turning towards me and immediately turning away, blushing all the while. Well, as much as a ghost could blush, I suppose. I might have just imagined that part.

I chuckled to myself and continued my morning routine. Even though I had only a spotty amount of hair on my face, I decided to give myself a quick shave just to make sure I had a completely clean-shaven look. After that, I put on a nice, white button up shirt, a black button up vest over the shirt, a clean pair of socks, and

28

my favorite pair of black khaki pants. I grabbed my cell phone, wallet, car keys, and Blue-tooth headset.

"It's fine, now. I'm fully dressed," I said.

"Are you sure?" My companion slowly turned towards me, and sighed with relief when she saw I was being honest.

"Anyway, are you going to tell me your name now? Do you remember your name?"

"Of course I remember my name. Why wouldn't I?" Her voice began to drift after she asked this question, as I stared at her smugly with my arms crossed. "Oh, right, because I'm dead and a ghost and everything. I do, though. It's Raquel Cobb."

"Nice to meet you, Raquel."

"Nice to meet you too, Vinnie."

I turned from the ghost as I started walking towards my kitchen. "Well, I'm going to make myself some breakfast. Do you want anything?" Before she could answer, I turned back around with my right index finger out, saying, "Kidding, kidding." I began walking down the stairs. "I've got to admit, Raquel," I said as she followed me down the stairs, "You are much more talkative than I expected you to be."

"What do you mean?"

"I just figured with the whole 'Why?' 'Why?' 'Why?' shtick last night you'd be much less willing to talk about things, that's all."

"Oh, that!" she giggled, as she darted through me

and in front of me, causing me to move back a little bit as she floated just in front of me, "That was just me goofing around. I thought since I was a ghost, it'd be more dramatic to do things that way. I mean, that's what ghosts are supposed to do, right? Moan about how they are dead?"

Shaking my head as I spoke, I walked past her and moved towards the kitchen. "I suppose, but next time I'd rather you just ask me directly."

"Let me ask you directly, then. Do you know why I died, Vinnie?"

"Please call me Vincent. I prefer Vincent—Vincent is an adult's name." I opened the refrigerator door and pulled out a couple of eggs and a loaf of bread. I also began brewing up some coffee.

"Oh, okay," she replied. "'Vincent.'" She made sure to deepen her voice and stress the Vincent. "I've got to make sure I say your name like an adult. Vincent. Do you know why I died?"

"Can't say I do," I confessed, as I began frying the eggs and toasting the bread. "But it's what I intend to find out."

"Sounds good. Can I trust you to do that for me though, Vinnie?" she said teasingly.

"Vincent."

"Oh, yes, 'Vincent.' Can I trust you to find out why I died?"

I chuckled at her comment. As I was about to place

my plate of food on the table, I realized that I had left the remnants of a solitaire game I was playing the previous night on the kitchen table. I swept the cards off the table with my free hand, and then had room to place the plate down. I moved towards the coffee pot that was finished boiling my coffee. Speaking to the ghost girl as I poured myself a cup, I said, "It's not like you really have much of a choice. I'm probably the only one in this city who can see you. Well, besides my mother." I placed the cup on the table and began eating my breakfast.

"Yeah, I noticed that when I tried to get people's attention on the streets. It was like I was invisible. Normally I don't have trouble getting men's attention." She shook her hips a bit as she said this and pointed at her chest. She giggled immediately after. "At least I didn't when I was alive."

I stopped chewing for a moment and scanned her face and body. It's difficult to tell specific features with a ghost, but she definitely had a nice figure and an alluring face. She appeared to be no older than her mid-twenties, though if you suggested younger than that, I wouldn't have been surprised. Alas, I thought to myself, the poor girl died young. I nodded my head. "You probably would have gotten my attention too."

"Oh, you're so sweet," she said, giggling as the words came out of her mouth. "For what it's worth, you are a very attractive man yourself, Vinnie."

"It's Vin— Oh, forget it. Yeah sure, I'm so attractive

31

the only woman in my life is my mother. Anyway, I'm pretty sure I'll be able to help you out. I've been doing it for a while, ever since I was a kid."

"Oh, so I'm not the first ghost you've ever met?"

"Hardly. I've lost track of all the ghosts I've met over the years."

"Do all ghosts want to find out why they died?"

"Not always. In fact, most ghosts I meet want me to resolve something for them, whether it be giving their child a toy as a memento of their undying love, or a trinket to confess a love or something to that effect. It usually involves love. Very rarely does a ghost visit me wanting to learn something much more mundane, like who won the World Series. I've got to admit, though, if a ghost ever woke me up and asked who won the World Series, that'd be pretty awesome."

"Who did win the World Series?"

"The Houston Astros."

"I didn't think they were that good."

"They've been pretty good for a while now."

"Eh, I'm not a big baseball fan."

"Too bad. For a second I thought that's why you were here. Then again, you didn't disappear, so it's pretty obvious that's not what you came for."

"Ghosts disappear? Where do they disappear to?"

"You don't know?"

"Am I supposed to?"

"I don't know. A ghost has never asked me before,

that's all."

"Imagine that—I'm the first ghost to ask this question. Are you sure I'm the first to ask you that question?"

"Quite sure. No ghost has ever asked me anything like that. Don't get me wrong, I've thought about what happens after a ghost disappears. I always assumed that a ghost's spirit went into the hereafter, or for lack of a better term, Heaven. Now that you mention it, though, I don't know that for certain. Frankly, I always believed a ghost just instinctively knew, like it was something that you just learned as soon as you died and became a ghost. I thought that's why I was never asked. Now I'm not sure what happens when you disappear."

"Maybe I'm the first ghost who doesn't know. Or maybe it's just something a ghost learns later on and something will jog it later. I don't know. Anyway, I understand, Vinnie. I suppose it's not that important."

"Perhaps it's just something you find out when the mystery is solved and you are about to move on. Speaking of which, just to confirm, you said you wanted to know why you died, correct?"

"That seems to be the case, yes."

"All right. That's actually the second most common reason a ghost visits me. Typically he or she or it wants to find out how and why they died and who killed them. Typically he, she, or it wants to know the full details of their deaths. Sometimes it's an accident, often it's on purpose, although sometimes it's just a guy or gal that accidentally killed his or herself. Sometimes it isn't accidental—those are always very sad."

"It sounds like you've figured out a lot of these mysteries, then."

"Absolutely. Solving mysteries is kind of my job."

"What do you do?"

"I'm a private investigator."

"Oh, like Sam Spade or Thomas Magnum." She began mimicking gun fire with her hands. "Bang! Bang! Pow! Pow!"

"No, nothing like that," I said, chuckling a bit. "I mostly deal with housewives trying to catch their husbands cheating, or I do due diligence investigations; making sure a company is on the level and isn't a risky investment, that sort of thing."

"Oh, that's disappointing," she said with a sigh. "Sounds kind of boring."

I shrugged as I sipped my coffee. "It pays the bills. The job also gives me good cover to do some investigative work for the ghosts that visit me every now and again. It's a lot easier to get to places if people think you have a reason for being there. I can't exactly tell them I'm doing investigative work for dead people."

"Why not? Oh, right, because nobody else can see them."

"Among other reasons, yes." Having emptied my coffee cup, I got out of my seat, mug still in hand, and headed towards the kitchen sink as I said, "Normally I'm swamped with clients. Luckily for you, I'm currently in between cases, so I'll have time to take care of you today."

She smirked as I set the coffee cup down in the sink. "Ah, yes. Of course. I'm sure people are usually beating down your door. Lucky me."

"Hey, do you want my help or don't you?"

"Okay, okay, I'm sorry." Her grin didn't leave her face.

"Come on, it's time to go."

"Go? Where are we going?"

"It sort of depends. Do you remember where you lived? Your home is usually a good place to start."

The ghost had a stern look on her face as she tried to recall, but after about a minute or so of attempted recollecting she had to confess, "No, I'm afraid I don't. I know I lived in this city, but that's about it."

"Well then, I suppose we'll head over to my mom's house."

"Mama's boy," she said teasingly.

"I don't want to visit her because I'm a mama's boy," I said with a smile and mock anger. "She's just a better medium than I am. She can tell just by looking at a ghost how long they've been dead. I'm afraid I can't do that, so you could have been dead from any range of times from this morning to several centuries ago."

"I assume the task will be much more difficult if I have been dead for centuries."

"The degree of difficulty would jump up immensely,

yes," I said. "But considering you're familiar with things like showers and Thomas Magnum, I'm assuming you're not from the colonial age."

"Probably not," she confirmed.

"I'm guessing it's a recent death. My mom will pinpoint it a little more exactly. I still don't know if you've been dead since yesterday or for several years."

"Is it that important to know my exact time of death?"

"Exact time, no, but knowing an approximate time could help us figure out our next move."

"Ah, like what to research, who to talk to, where a good place to look might be, things like that, right?"

"Exactly. Besides, you asked earlier about what happens when ghosts disappear. Mom's been doing this a lot longer than I have, and frankly, she's just better at this than me. Maybe she knows what happens."

"Well, it seems like visiting your mom is a very good idea, then."

"It's a place to start at least."

"By the way, your mother never taught you the ability to find out a ghosts' age? Or is it an ability you are born with?"

"She's tried to teach me," I confessed, my hand rubbing the back of my neck as I said this. "But to tell the truth, I could never quite understand what she was trying to teach me."

"Do you get along with your mother?"

"I'd say so, yeah—for the most part, at least. We have

our moments, like any mother and son do, but nothing too serious."

"That's good to hear. I know I teased you, but I seem to recall that I had a good relationship with my mother and my father, so I think it's great that you get along with her so well."

"That's kind of you to say. Thank you very much."

"Hey, Vinnie?"

"Yeah?"

"Don't you find it odd that I can remember things like my name, Thomas Magnum, and what a private investigator is, but I can't remember things like my home address? Is that typical of ghosts?"

"Actually, it is very common. From my experience, the best way to describe a ghost's memory is it is like Swiss cheese, and it is almost completely random what you remember and what you don't. However, most ghosts tend to forget the more important facets of their lives, like their friends, their address, what they did for a living, their home and family life, and other important things like that. Trauma also has an impact on a ghost's memory. Let's say a ghost was a racecar driver who was killed in a car crash. The ghost might forget that he was a racecar driver, what a racecar is, what the significance of his racing gloves was, or even that he once knew how to drive. It seems that a ghost is subconsciously refusing to remember those sorts of things for whatever reason. Even showing him those items may not jog his memory until we actually reach the track where he crashed. Even then, a 'ghost whisperer' like me might have to meticulously explain what happened to the ghost before he can figure out how he died."

"I see. So you can never be sure why I might not remember something. It is just so very frustrating. It feels like my head is in a fog. It's like I can see the memory off in the distance and can make out its basic shape, but I cannot quite see the face."

"Don't worry. Like I said, that's pretty typical, and these memories tend to come back, especially if or when you see something familiar to you such as friends and family, a toy you might have liked as a kid, a reminder of where you used to work, basically anything that might have been important to you in the past. Typically these memories come rushing back, too. To use your metaphor, you'll be able to recognize the face the closer you get to the memory. Some things anyway. For others, you might need an interpreter, for lack of a better term. Someone to gather up evidence to help you remember things. Luckily for you, that's what I'm here for."

I pulled out my Bluetooth ear piece and placed it over my left ear.

"Planning on making a phone call?" my ghostly companion asked. "See? It's very frustrating. I know what a Bluetooth headset and cell phone are, but I don't know how old I am. Or, I guess I should say 'was,' considering—you know, I died."

"Like I said, don't get discouraged, the memories will come back. It's just a side effect of being a ghost. Anyway, this ear piece is for subterfuge," I explained. "It makes it easier for me to talk to ghosts. People tend to stare at you less when they see you talking to yourself if they think you're actually talking to someone on the phone."

"Ah, very clever. Wait—what happens if someone calls you or texts you while you're talking to a ghost? Won't that give you away?"

"Luckily, it hasn't happened to me yet. Besides, if it happens in my car or even out in public most people won't really notice. This provides cover in situations such as…well, let's say I'm meeting someone and they arrive five or ten minutes late, but I'm in the middle of talking to a ghost when that person arrives. If I tell them I was talking to someone on the phone it doesn't arouse any suspicion."

"That sounds like a very specific example."

"Like I told you, I've been doing this for a while. Some of the things I do now are based off of personal experience. Anyway, let's get out of here." I went into the living room and grabbed my black and silver briefcase that I had placed next to my brown, faux-leather couch.

"My, don't we look professional," Raquel humorously said.

"It looks more professional than the backpack I used to carry around," I admitted. "I usually put clues and

39

other things I find on my cases in here. Right now all I have in here are a couple of pens and a notebook I use to take down testimonies during cases."

"Not using a phone or a tablet or a laptop to take down that information?"

"I guess I'm old school that way. Besides, a notebook is a lot easier to carry around and maneuver. Laptops are a little too clunky, and it's difficult for me to write quickly on a phone or tablet. While I sometimes use the phone to record voices, most of the time my notes are all I need."

Raquel shrugged. "Okay, makes sense to me. I was just curious."

"No problem. Anyway, let's get out of here."

With that, I signaled to the ghost to follow me as I opened the front door. My car was in the driveway, as I use my garage mostly for storage.

I was next to my 2010 Blue Honda Civic that had scratch marks all over, pulling out my keys, when I realized I had lost track of my companion. I looked around, to my left, to my right, but I just could not see her anywhere. "Raquel," I muttered to myself. "Where did you go?"

"Boo!"

"Jesus Christ in Heaven!" I screamed, dropping my briefcase. The ghost girl had appeared before me having floated from underneath my car, after having apparently disappeared from my sight by going underneath the pavement.

"Don't come in here," she said, wobbling her voice as she spoke. "This car is haunted by a ghost! A very, very sexy ghost!" She started cracking up. Her laugh was high pitched and jovial, much like you'd expect from a young woman her age. It didn't have the haunted tone and tenor you'd think an apparition would have.

"Why did you do that?" I yelled. "You scared the shit out of me!"

"I thought it'd be funny, and it was. You should have seen yourself, it was hilarious. Your arms were flailing all over the place. I thought you were going to fall right on your ass."

I scowled at the girl. "Just get out of my seat, Raquel."

"Why don't you sit on my lap?" she said with her index finger to her lip as she wore a coy smile. I continued to glare at her. She started laughing once again. "Oh, I'm just being silly, Vinnie. I'm pretty sure you couldn't sit on my lap even if you wanted to. Besides, isn't it more appropriate for a girl to sit on the guy's lap? Not that I can do that either."

"Additionally," I said, shooing her away from my seat, "It's weird touching ghosts."

"Why? What's it like touching a ghost?" she asked, as she finally complied and floated over to the passenger seat.

"It's a little hard to describe," I said as I entered the car, tossing my briefcase in the back seat. "It kind of feels

41

like your hand or other body part is being covered in insects, very tiny insects. It's also feels cold, absolutely freezing in fact. It's like touching a block of ice. I hate the cold. We're in the middle of November too, it's just going to get colder." I began backing the car out of the driveway.

"Um, you're going to have to float along with the car," I said, stopping the car for a second as I noticed her staying in place, floating a few inches in front of the passenger seat as I backed up. "You are, after all, a non-corporeal being."

"Right. God, I keep forgetting about things like that," she said, as she floated backwards into her seat.

"You don't have to sit next to me. You can just float next to me or next to the car or something, or just follow me around. That's what most ghosts do."

"No, no, it's easy enough for me to float as if I were sitting next to you, as long as I concentrate on it. I want to talk to you, and it's easier to do it if I'm right here. Besides, it makes me feel more human."

"Okay, if that's the way you feel."

"Non-corporeal," she snickered. "Did you get that from your word of the day app or something?"

"I think I heard it in a movie," I confessed. I began backing the car out once again.

"So," she continued. "Does it feel weird when I do this?" She put her left arm through my chest.

I immediately slammed on the brakes. Fortunately, I

was still in my driveway at the time. "Jeez Louise, why do you keep doing things like that?"

"Hmm. For me it's about the same as usual. Imagine that."

"Would you please take your hand out of me right now? It's freezing!"

"Oh, right. Sorry," she said sheepishly, and removed her hand from my chest. "I didn't notice anything different, though."

After taking a couple of deep breaths to recover a bit, I backed my car up onto the main road and began driving down to the police station, her floating in the passenger's seat right beside me.

"What do you mean by that?" I asked. "You didn't notice anything different?"

"It didn't feel any different when I touched you just now. I thought touching a person would feel a little bit different for me, but it feels the same as touching anything else."

"Oh yeah? How does it feel when you touch things?"

"It's difficult to describe, but it's not so much I actually feel something as much as I feel its presence. It's like I can feel something around me or around my hand or around my body, but I can't actually touch anything, if that makes any sense at all."

"I think I understand. At least, as much as I could possibly understand. It sounds pretty surreal, if you ask me."

43

"It is, but you get used to it pretty quickly, honestly."

"I have to admit, if I didn't know any better, I'd think you were actually sitting down in my passenger seat. Most ghosts would give up and just float next to the car, not remain seated next to me. I've been told that floating in a sitting motion is very uncomfortable."

"Whoever told you that was correct. I'm actually concentrating very hard to keep it up."

"Like I said, you don't have to sit next to me, you know."

"I like sitting next to you, though," she said, and flashed me a big grin.

"Thank you. I'm very flattered," I said, and flashed a grin back. Both of us laughed at our own silliness, and continued to banter a bit until we arrived at my mother's house.

We drove into the paved driveway of the brick home and I parked my car in front of the smoky gray garage door. I took out my Bluetooth as we passed by the green and yellow lawn and walked to the brown, laminated doors. I rang the doorbell. After a few seconds, a woman with smoky hair worn in a medium layered haircut, wearing a tight blue shirt and with a floral printed unbuttoned, fleece jacket and long black pants, appeared in front of me.

"Hi Mom!" I said. I quickly realized she was still on the phone when she greeted me.

"I'm afraid I'm going to have to call you back, Shirley.

Well, my only son decided to visit me today. I know, it is a rare event. It should be a national holiday or something. Oh yes, we're definitely on for bridge with Nicole and Beth tonight. Okay, well, talk to you soon." My mother hung up and placed her cell phone in her back pocket. "Sorry about that, Vincent, I didn't think you would visit me today. To what do I owe this pleasure?" My mother's head quickly turned to my ghostly companion. "Oh, you had another visit from a ghost, and you need your mother's help again. God forbid that you ever visit your mother just for the sake of visiting her."

"Ah, Mom, you know I've been busy lately. Besides, I visit you whenever I meet a ghost, don't I?"

"Yeah, because you can't analyze a ghost by yourself and you need your mother's help. Anyway, don't just stand there. Both of you, come in, come in."

We entered the door and followed my mother to the kitchen. I sat down on a stool as my mother leaned on one of the kitchen counters. "Well, Vincent? Aren't you going to introduce me to your friend?"

"The ghost is named Raquel Cobb."

"Raquel. Raquel is such an exotic name, perfect for such a lovely girl as you."

"Raquel isn't that rare of a name anymore, Mom," I interjected.

My mother ignored me and continued. "Except you do have that large gash on the top of your head. Funny, ghosts normally don't keep their wounds. Such a shame

45

too. But don't worry, it doesn't tarnish your beauty whatsoever."

"Thank you very much, Mrs. Pietro. You are an incredibly beautiful woman yourself. It's hard to believe that Vinnie is your son."

"Oh, stop!" my mother said in a falsely modest manner. "You are a very kind girl, Raquel, but I must ask you to please call me Vanessa. I feel so old when you call me Mrs. Pietro."

"You certainly don't look old, Vanessa. You look more like Vinnie's sister than his mother."

"Flattery will get you everywhere, Raquel. But thank you all the same. It is such a pleasure to meet you."

"It is a pleasure to meet you too."

"You see, Vinnie? This is the kind of girl that I'd like you to marry."

"Well, maybe when I find her corpse I'll propose to her."

"Vincent, that wasn't funny. Don't speak that way, especially not in front of our guest! Apologize to Raquel right now!"

"Mom, I was only joking," I protested.

"Now!" my mother said sternly.

"I'm a grown man, Mom, you can't make me—"

"NOW!"

"I'm sorry, Raquel," I said sheepishly. The ghost laughed in response.

"Whatever happened to that one girl you were

46

dating? What was her name, Kaley?"

"Oh, Kathy? Yeah, let's just say things didn't work out."

"What was wrong with her? I liked her all right."

"Mom, Kathy was weird. She was obsessed with identity politics. Declared herself to be a gender fluid and queer communist libertarian, whatever that means. Plus, she died her hair seaweed green. I hate that."

"Oh, she was weird? The boy who sees ghosts says that a girl's too weird for him. Still, I agree with you. She was a weird girl. I could never understand a single word out of her mouth either, now that I think about it. She kept talking about privilege too. Anyway, Vincent, I just want you to find someone, that's all. Or at least, I wish you had more of a social life. I had a wonderful social life when I was your age. What am I saying? I still have a great social life."

"Well, maybe—" I bit my tongue, barely stopping myself from putting my proverbial foot in my mouth by saying "Maybe you had too much of a social life, especially when I was a kid."

"Maybe what?" my mother said crossly.

"Maybe you're right, Mom," I said, and my mother's expression immediately softened. "I'll try to get out and socialize more. It's just tough sometimes with my schedule. It seems like I'm always working on a case or working with a ghost."

"You'd rather hang out with your ghost friends than

your own mother, then?"

"You know that's not true, Mom. You know I don't even particularly like ghosts."

"Oh, so you'd rather hang out with some ghosts you hate than your own mother then!"

"You know that's not true either, Mom! God, why do you say things like that when you know it's not true?"

"I just want you to visit me more often, Vincent."

"And I would, Mom, if I weren't so busy all the time! It's very difficult for me to even find time to relax. I have ghosts on my tail making me do things for them all the time. It's a very stressful job, Mom! You should know! You go through it too!"

"I know it can be tough, Vincent. Believe me, I do." My mother stared listlessly to the ground for a moment. I realized I had momentarily forgotten that she also went through the same types of trials and tribulations I did with ghosts, and I might literally be the only person in the world she had to talk to about such things.

"I'm sorry, Mom," I said. "I'll try to visit you more often, and talk to you more as well. I forget sometimes it can be difficult for you to have this 'gift' too."

"I know you don't have the easiest schedule in the world, and I know our 'gift' sometimes makes it tough for us to meet people. Still, I just worry about you, that's all. You always seem so focused on your work."

"I'll try to not be so obsessed with work in the future, Mom. I promise. Speaking of work, though, could you help me out?"

With a heavy sigh, my mother answered, "What do you need, Vincent?"

"Could you tell me how long this ghost has been dead?" I asked, pointing my finger at my ghostly acquaintance.

"Are you kidding? I can tell from a glance; she's been dead for at most a few days."

"How do you know that, Vanessa?" the ghost asked.

"It's very simple—and Vincent, you ought to pay attention to this now. Notice the shade of white she is...."

I have to be honest. At this point, I began to mentally check out as my mother went into an in-depth explanation as to how to figure out how long ago a person had died. I know it's something I should learn, but my mother goes into such detail and describes the process in such a dry manner that it makes it very easy for me to stop paying attention and start thinking about what my next step should be—or, quite honestly, the latest football scores or the women I've known in my life.

"...reading the aura, it makes it very simple for me to assess the time of her demise."

"Great! Thanks, Mom!"

"So you understood everything I said this time."

"Of course! I hung on your every word."

"Uh huh. So you won't need me next time. You can figure out the age of a ghost on your own, now."

"Well, I mean, I'll always want your expert opinion,

Mom."

My mother let out a heavy sigh. "I don't know who you think you are fooling, Vincent. You will never learn this, and you will never learn because you never pay any attention whenever I try to teach you these things."

"I'm sorry, Mom. It's just hard to learn something like this, especially from one lecture."

"I have books, Vincent. Our family has a lot of this written down. Our ancestors wanted to pass this knowledge along to us, and you refuse to learn. I tell you," she said, looking at the hovering apparition, "This boy never pays attention to his mother. He never wants to perfect his craft. He always has an excuse for everything. Why he can't learn, why he can't do something for me, why he can't visit me more often."

"Well, I'm sorry, Mom. It's hard to sit down in class or read a thousand-page book when I'm busy trying to put a ghost's spirit to rest all the time."

"Do you see what I have to deal with?" my mother said to the specter.

The spirit laughed in response. "Personally, I think he's just embarrassed that he can't learn and doesn't want to admit it."

"Perhaps you are right. We'll talk about this later, Vincent," my mother said, directing her attention back at me. "Anyway, it appears that Raquel's only been gone for a few days at most. I hope that information helps you out."

"If she's only been dead a few days," I said, "There's a chance that nobody but us even knows she's dead. Assuming she has family and friends, though, they have probably noticed she's missing by now."

"Assuming I have friends or family?" the ghost protested, hands on her hips. "Why wouldn't I have family, or at least friends?"

"Hey, I didn't mean anything by it, honestly. I just learned not to assume," I said in response.

"You can probably assume she has friends, Vincent. Even you have friends," my mother said. Raquel giggled in response.

"Mom," I whined, though admittedly I couldn't help but chuckle a little bit. "Anyway," I said, "Since it's a recent death, I might be able to get some information from Ed."

"Oh, Ed! I like Ed. Tell him I said hi," my mother said.

"Ed? Who's Ed?" asked the ghost.

"Ed Bergeron is a desk sergeant for the Tacoma Police Department. He's a good friend of mine. I can ask him if there have been any missing persons reports filed recently, and if not, if there were any deaths or murders or anything else similar. It'll help get the ball rolling, at least, since you can't seem to remember anything about where you lived, Raquel. Speaking of which, can you remember anything about where you used to live yet?"

"No, sorry. Still blank."

"Okay, then I think we'll head to the police station downtown. Mom, thank you for all of your help."

"I didn't help you all that much. I just told you a ghost's age. As I said, it's something you need to learn how to do by yourself."

"You're probably right, Mom."

"Come see me after your case is over. We'll go over how you can figure out how long a ghost has been dead. And Vincent?"

"Yeah, Mom?"

"Please visit me a little more often, not just when you have a ghost. It'd be nice to talk to you a little more often, okay? And you know you can always come to me if you have a problem, right?"

"I know, Mom. I will. I should get going now, though." I signaled to the ghost floating in the kitchen. "Raquel, let's go." I turned towards my mother. "Thanks again, and take care." I then gave her a hug before I left, which solicited an "aww" from the apparition. "I'll see you later, Mom."

"Goodbye, Vincent," my mother said.

We started to head towards the exit, when suddenly the ghost turned around and shouted, "Oh wait! Just before we go, I have to ask you something!"

"Okay," my mother said, a little taken aback. "What do you want to ask?"

"Vinnie didn't know the answer to this question, but I hope you do. What happens when a ghost disappears?"

"Huh. Funny, a ghost has never actually asked me that before."

"I know, right?" I said.

"Frankly, I always assumed a ghost knew, like when they are roaming around someone or something tells them what will happen to them after they disappear, which explained why we were never asked."

"That's what I said!"

"There's been a lot of speculation, of course. Most of us, as in most members of our family, believe you will go to Heaven or somewhere equivalent. But honestly, we're not sure. We always assumed since there are spirits there must be some sort of afterlife, but that's about the extent of what we know."

"Hey! I guess I knew more than I thought," I said, more delighted than I should have been with this revelation.

"Okay," the ghost said meekly. "Thank you, Vanessa."

"Don't worry, Raquel, I'm sure you'll be going to a better place. A kind, gentle spirit such as yourself should have nothing to worry about."

"Thank you very much, Vanessa! You are way too kind!"

"No problem. As I said before, if either of you have any questions please do not hesitate to ask."

"Thanks, Mom. Anyway, we better get going." This time we were able to leave without any issues.

The ghost and I entered the car, and as I sat down on

my seat and she floated over to hers, she immediately began to converse. "I think your mother is simply wonderful. She was so nice!"

Placing my phone in the charger and putting on my Bluetooth, I said to her, "Yeah, my mother's all right. She's a good person, and a good mother."

"An entire family that can see ghosts—imagine that! Is your family the only ones who can see ghosts?"

"Probably not in the world, but definitely in this city. Yeah, I would say that's true. At the very least, I haven't met anybody else who can see ghosts. At least, not anybody who would admit it." I started the car and backed out of the driveway, and began my journey to the police station.

"Vinnie, I couldn't help but notice something when you and your mother were talking."

"Yeah?"

"You said you didn't particularly like helping out ghosts. Is this true?"

I stumbled over my words a bit. "Well, I mean, it's not as if I truly hate ghosts or anything, and I don't necessarily hate the idea of helping them, and from what I could tell you seem like a nice ghost and everything—"

"Vinnie," my ghostly companion interrupted. "It's okay. You can be honest with me."

"I absolutely abhor helping ghosts. Most of the time at least."

"Why?"

"Some of it is just the idea of ghosts appearing at random to me, and that my mother and I are the only ones who can see you. It is exasperating having such an ability, and literally having only one other person to talk to about it who understands what you are going through."

"The only one to talk to besides ghosts, you mean?" she said, with a meek smile.

"Not really, no. They don't talk either, most of the time at least," I confessed. "No ghost I've ever previously met ever made small talk or showed much care for me at all. I was a tool for them, a means to an end. Now that you mention it, every other ghost I've talked to was obsessed with their one goal. All they would talk about was their loved one, what they wanted accomplished, finding out how and why they died, that sort of thing. For most ghosts it's like prying teeth to get any information out of them. You're not like any other ghost I've ever seen or talked to before."

"I knew I was special," she said, wearing a fatuous smile.

"You really are. In many ways, you are completely unique. For example, you're the only one that's ever shown any concern for me at all."

"Are you serious?"

"Yeah, I'm afraid so. A lot of ghosts I've met are pretty unpleasant to talk to, and have a sour disposition. They are probably a little aggravated about being dead.

I can't really blame them too much for that; I'd probably be the same way. Still, when someone refuses to talk to me or tells me to shut up and focus on the task, it makes it very difficult for me to want to help them out."

"Yeah, of course it would! It must be awful to have to help out so many hostile and ungrateful spirits."

"I wouldn't describe most ghosts as hostile—more like aloof. In fact, even though I've met my fair share of disagreeable spirits, the majority of ghosts aren't particularly nasty towards me. Most are polite and courteous, they just have a singular focus and aren't very grateful. Take a ghost I knew named Casper, for instance."

"Casper?"

"Yeah, Casper Jenkins. He was all right."

"Would you then say, then, he was a 'friendly ghost'?" she said with a wry smile.

"He was nice enough, I suppose.... Oh, wait a minute. You're talking about the cartoon, aren't you?"

"Yes!" She started giggling as I sighed deeply. "I'm sorry, I'm sorry, go on. Continue, please."

"Anyway, Casper was a lot like you, a ghost who just wanted to find out why he died. He was the first I met who was like that. He was a decent enough fellow, for the most part."

"Why did he die?"

"Wife shot him."

"Oh! It must have been an accident, though, right?"

"Wow. Actually, you hit the nail right on the head. Good guess. He was playing a prank on her. She thought he was an intruder. Shot him blindly before figuring out who he was. The good man even forgave his wife before he disappeared. Still, he never thanked me."

"He didn't thank you? But you helped him out."

"He just disappeared. He had time to thank me, too, but instead just talked to his wife as he faded into the ether."

"That was rude of him. I know he had other things on his mind, but still, he should have at least thanked you for helping him out."

"That's all I'm saying! Finally, someone agrees with me. My mother thinks I'm crazy for expecting gratitude. It's nice to find someone who agrees with me."

Suddenly, Raquel's voice took on a more serious tenor. "Vinnie?"

"Yes? Is something the matter?"

"I promise to thank you before I go."

I smiled and snickered a bit. "I appreciate it. We'll see what happens when the time comes."

"No, I'm serious, I will thank you."

I smiled. "Okay, then. Thank you." Chortling a bit as I spoke, I continued, "Like I keep saying, Raquel, you are a ghost unlike any other."

After a short, contemplative pause by the specter sitting next to me, the ghost began to speak once again.

"Why do you help them out, then?"

"Hmm?"

"The ghosts, I mean. Why do you help them out?"

"That's a good question. I've thought about the same thing myself many times throughout the years, and I haven't quite come up with an answer. I'm afraid I don't have time to think about it now, though," I said, pulling my vehicle parallel to a car parked next to the side of the road. "We're just about there."

"Already?"

"Yeah, the police station isn't too far from where my mother lives, and I do need a second to parallel park, and admittedly I need all the concentration I can get to do this." The ghost remained silent as I parallel parked next to the police station. I then exited the car, locked the car doors, and asked Raquel to follow me. "It's time to meet Ed," I said.

CHAPTER 3

A short drive is all it took for us to arrive at the station. We walked up the white steps through the glass door under the sign that had the word "Police" written in dark blue. The building had a rustic smell to it with its white brick slowly changing to a grungy yellow, as the police station had been there for several decades now and a lack of funding had caused maintenance to be a bit neglected.

A rotund man with receding brown hair and a somber yet gentle face was working at the desk. Upon seeing me he stood up, greeting me warmly and waving his hand as he said, "Vince! It's good to see you!"

I waved back, smiling broadly. "Ed! It's good to see you too! It's been awhile."

"Hey, it's good to see ya in a good mood for once, Vince! Life treating ya well lately?"

"Not bad, I suppose. Could be better, could be worse."

"Good to hear. How's yer mother doing?"

"Oh, she's fine. I actually visited her just before I got here. She says hi, by the way."

"I'm glad to hear she's doing good. Be sure to tell her that I said hello too."

A feminine voice whispered in my ear. "Oh sure, he's allowed to call you Vince, but I can't call you Vinnie?"

I turned towards my left shoulder to speak to my female companion, making numbers with my right hand as I said, "First, you call me Vinnie. You actually haven't stopped calling me Vinnie. And two, Ed and I have history together. We've known each other for years. And three, I prefer Vince to Vinnie. Vince doesn't bother me so much."

"Whatever you say, Vinnie," she responded, shrugging ostentatiously as she said this.

"Um, who ya talkin' to, Vince?" Ed asked, clearly perplexed.

I turned towards Ed and tapped my Bluetooth headset in my left ear. "Sorry about that, Ed. I was talking to a friend of mine before I walked in here, and she seems to still be on the line. I meant to hang up on her, but apparently I did not."

Raquel whispered in my ear. "I guess wearing that thing really is good cover."

"See," I whispered back. "I know what I'm doing. I've been doing this a long time."

"Ah, that makes sense," Ed said. "You can finish that conversation if ya want. I'll wait for ya."

"Nah, it's okay Ed, I'll finish up," I said. "Yeah, listen, I'm talking to a good friend right now, so I'm afraid I'm going to have to call you back."

"No!" Raquel shouted, covering her mouth in a modest attempt to cover up her laughter. "You must talk to me and to me only! I'm the only one you are allowed to talk to!"

I scowled at her as I continued, "Glad you understand. Goodbye." And with that, I mocked hanging up on my phantom companion.

"Everything okay?" Ed asked, "You looked sullen there for a moment. Hope I didn't cost ya anything with that young lady."

"Oh. Uh, not at all. She's just a friend."

"Well, that's too bad. I'm sure you'll find someone soon."

I nodded in appreciation as I said, "Thanks, Ed."

"In the meantime, you might as well concentrate on yer work. How's that been treating ya? Have ya had a lot of clients lately?"

"Actually, that's kind of why I'm here."

"Yeah, I kinda figured," Ed said with a sigh. "I didn't think this was just a social visit."

"Sorry, I'm afraid not, Ed. I wanted to know if you've had any missing persons reports lately."

"Are ya looking for something fer a client?"

"Not quite. Looking to see if I can dig up any clients."

"How do ya figure ya can do that with a missin'

persons report?"

"Honestly, my plan is to visit people who have filed missing persons reports and offer my services."

"Wow, really? That's yer plan? Business has been that bad lately?"

"I'm afraid so."

"Wow. Well, that is public information. You could look it up online if ya really wanted to."

"Yeah, but if I did that, I wouldn't have been able to see my favorite police officer. It's been a while since I visited you."

"Hey, thanks, Vince. That's awfully kind of ya ta say. Anyway, just give me a sec to see if I can find anything fer ya. How far back do ya want to go?"

"Within the last week would be fine."

Ed sat down and began typing furiously as I leaned on his desk and exchanged some trivial small talk with the man as he looked up the desired information. After a few minutes, he said, "Well, we've only had one missin' persons report in the last week. At least the only one in this area. I can look back further if ya want."

"That may not be necessary. Who's the missing person?"

"A Miss Raquel Cobb, twenty years old. Her parents reported her missin' yesterday afternoon."

"Who is the investigating officer on this case?"

"I believe it is Kelly Martinez."

"Would he be able to provide any insight?"

"I don't think he's actually had the chance to speak with the parents yet."

"Why not?"

"Ya know how it is, Vince. Martinez has like three other cases he's working on, including a homicide down by the Port of Tacoma. He had ta prioritize. She'll probably show up after a few days. I mean, she's twenty years old — she's probably just out there enjoying life, and her overprotective parents are simply overreactin'." Ed sighed heavily and his head lowered, almost as if he was reminiscing or felt some remorse. "Either that, or her body will be found. In which case we'll escalate the case quite a bit."

I reacted to Ed's comments by wincing a bit and biting my tongue. Though what Ed said was correct, I felt a little angry — perhaps because I felt Ed's comments were a bit callous, but more likely because I already knew Raquel's fate, and thought for a moment that perhaps if more had been done, the young woman would still be with us today.

I quickly dismissed those thoughts, though. Raquel was reported missing a day ago, but likely had died longer ago than that. Plus, there was only so much human beings could do, and preventing crime was no easy task. Frankly, an officer's job often was not to prevent crime as much as it was to deal with the aftermath.

I reminded myself that officers had to deal with a multitude of cases at one time, and it was not as if Martinez was ignoring the case, he just had other priorities. Besides, if nothing else, it was not as if any of this was Ed's fault, and he obviously felt badly about the reality of the situation. Thus, after a deep breath to calm myself a bit, I tried to lighten the mood.

"I understand, Ed. That makes sense. You're right, she'll probably show up soon, but in the meantime, I guess I can investigate the case a little," I said, rubbing the back of my neck. "By the way, you told me she was reported missing yesterday. You don't remember filing a report yesterday? Ed, you really are getting old."

"Hey! It was my day off yesterday! And I ain't that old, I'm only forty-two!"

"You mean you're already forty-two," I said with a chuckle. "Still, I wish I had known it was your day off — we could have found something to do."

"Would ya have really wanted to spend the afternoon with an old man like me?" he snarled.

"I was just kidding, Ed — I didn't think you were so sensitive."

"If ya really want to do something with me, why don't ya come over to the house for poker night this Saturday? Some of the boys from the precinct will be over, and I think you'll get along with them great. Most of them are around your age, anyway, so you'll probably have more in common with them than even me. It should be a fun time."

"I'll think about it, Ed. I'm not really a big poker

player."

"It's just fer fun, Vince. We don't play fer money, just chips. Think about it, all right?"

"Okay, I'll think about it. You still haven't told me what you were doing yesterday."

"Oh, right. I spent the day with Stacey yesterday. It was her birthday."

"Wow, so it was little Stacey's birthday yesterday. How old is she now?"

"Twelve years old. They really do grow up too fast, ya know?"

"How come you didn't invite me?"

"I think yer a little old to be attending a twelve-year-old's birthday party. Age-wise, not maturity wise."

"Very funny, wise guy. I just meant the two of us could have hung out."

"I know, but it really was just a day for my daughter. All my attention was spent catering to her and her friends' needs. I tell ya, it was quite a long day. Since Lori isn't around anymore to help us out with those kind of things, it was up to me and Cindy to take care of all of Stacey's needs."

"Oh yeah, how is Lori doing?"

"Very good. Just started her freshman year in college. She seems to be adjusting pretty good to school life—much better than my wife, at least. I keep telling Cindy she has to stop calling her every day. Lori needs to learn how to be independent, but she just yells at me and then ignores me. A husband's lot in life, you know? It's funny. Cindy was freakin' out last night because she thinks Lori's already met a guy. I keep telling Cindy she's eighteen, she's plenty old for a boyfriend, but Cindy keeps thinkin' of her as — well, a little girl Stacey's age, not a young adult."

"Lori's found a man? That's too bad, I was going to ask you if you'd be okay with me asking her out sometime," I said with a broad grin.

"Vinnie."

"Even if you did ask her out, I wouldn't allow it. Not with someone like you, leastways. Besides, there's no way she would go out with you — she has standards." He then chuckled. "Ah, just messin' with ya — you know I love ya."

"If you loved me, why wouldn't you want me to be your son-in-law?"

"We'd be here all day if I had to list all the reasons," he said, stifling his laughter. "Least of which, ain't you a little bit too old for her?"

"What do you mean? A five-year age difference isn't that big of a deal, is it?"

"Vinnie!"

Ed began rubbing his beard. "Christ, that's right — I keep forgettin' yer only twenty-three. Ya really are just a kid."

"VINNIE!"

"What? What is it? Why are you shouting at

me?" I turned towards my left shoulder and saw the consternation on Raquel's face.

"I wasn't shoutin', Vince," Ed said, a look of confusion plastered on his face. "I just forgot you were that much younger than me, that's all. I was just a bit surprised. Sorry if I upset you."

"Oh—uh," I stuttered, trying to come up with something to excuse my strange behavior. "I'm sorry, Ed. It's just...it's just been very stressful for me lately. You know, I haven't had a lot of clients, and it has really been stressing me out. I didn't get much sleep last night, either, so I must be imagining things."

"Vinnie, why are you ignoring me?" Raquel whined.

"Look, I just wanted to have a conversation with a really good friend of mine," I growled back at her.

"Uh, yeah, I know," Ed said, worry beginning to creep up in his face. "That's what I was doing. I hope I didn't offend ya with the immaturity comments or nothin'. I was just goofing around. Ya know me; ya know I do that all the time. Normally doesn't bother ya."

"Ah, jeez, I'm sorry again, Ed," I said as I made another attempt to profusely apologize. "I've just—I mean—ah, I'm just sorry, Ed."

My friend let out a heavy sigh. "It's okay, kid. It's okay. Look, why don't I just print ya out the missin' persons report on Raquel Cobb, and I can send ya on your way? Her address is printed on there. You can visit her family if you want. They probably have more information than I can provide."

"Thanks Ed," I said, with an equally heavy sigh. "Again, I am really sorry."

Ed made a hand gesture as if to say, "Don't worry about it," but I couldn't help but think I had greatly upset my friend. By this point, Raquel was shouting all sorts of things in my ear with the basic theme of justifying her behavior—this time I was able to ignore her. Ed and I remained silent as he printed out the missing persons report and handed it to me.

"Here," he said. "This should be enough information to send ya on yer way."

"Thanks Ed," I said, taking the sheets of paper embarrassedly. "I'll, uh, see you later, Ed."

"Yeah. It was good seeing you." I gave him an awkward wave as I turned and headed out the door.

"Well," I said as I entered the car, putting the phone in the charger. "I'm sure Ed thinks I'm insane now."

"I'm sorry, Vinnie," Raquel said, entering the car and sitting next to me again.

"What was so important that it couldn't wait another five or ten minutes?"

"Oh, I think it had something to do with his daughter? Something about his daughter sparked something in my memory, I think. Imagine that, I must have forgotten completely," she said, smiling guiltily. "I'm sorry, Vinnie."

I left my hands on the steering wheel and my keys in

the ignition as I stared off into the distance. "Something to do with his daughter," I muttered, loudly enough that Raquel could hear me. "That's just great. I'm sure whatever it was it would have been the lynchpin of this case. Maybe it was Lori that was responsible for your demise, or maybe it was little Stacey. Yes, Stacey probably took a sledgehammer and bludgeoned your head. Mystery solved, goodbye Raquel."

"Vinnie, that's so mean!" Raquel said with her voice cracking.

"Oh my God," I said, reaching out to the girl with my right hand, momentarily forgetting I couldn't literally place my hand on her shoulder. "Oh, God, that's still cold!" I shouted, moving my hand in the air and back down to my side, Raquel staring at my hand the entire time. "Raquel," I said. "I am so sorry. I didn't mean it, I shouldn't have said that."

"I'm sorry too, Vinnie," she said. "I didn't mean to interrupt your conversation with Ed."

"Normally, I don't mind if people think I'm insane," I explained. "But Ed Bergeron is a really good friend. He's one of my closest friends. He's also helped me quite a bit over the years, and is basically an exemplary human being. Still, God, what I said was so cruel." I let out a heavy sigh. "Sometimes I forget how difficult things must be for you. I admit that I can be very selfish at times, perhaps even too jaded. I forget sometimes that I'm talking to a person—or at least, a person's ghost. Honestly, I can't

69

even imagine how you must feel right now."

"It's not so bad," Raquel said, smiling. "At least I found someone to help me."

"That's kind of you to say. More than I deserve, right now, to be honest."

"It's not all your fault, though, Vinnie. I should have waited before yelling in your ear. I can be a little annoying at times, I know."

"Regardless, I'll try harder to keep your feelings in mind from now on, okay?"

"Okay, Vinnie." We both exchanged grins. "Anyway," Raquel continued, "Aren't you going to take a look at that missing persons report?"

"Oh right, almost forgot I had that thing. I'd better take a look."

I carefully examined the report. At the top of the report was a picture of a young woman. I couldn't help but notice that the woman had a truly captivating face.

"I assume this is you, Raquel?" I asked, showing her the picture.

"Let me see. Oh yes, mm-hmm," confirmed Raquel.

With that, I nodded and continued gazing at the photograph. She really had been a beautiful girl. In the photograph, Raquel had fair white skin with heavy, coal black eyeliner around the eyes and dark, ruby red lipstick. Her brunette hair hung down to her shoulders with slight curls at the bottom. Raquel's warm, green eyes and alluring smile made me wish I had known this

70

girl while she was alive.

"Were you really into the gothic look?" I asked.

"I think so. I think it was just something I was into when I was in high school that continued after I graduated. If I remember correctly, I was actually getting kind of tired of it, and was planning on changing my makeup style soon."

"That would have been a shame, because it really looks good on you."

"Let me take another look." I showed her the picture once again. "Well, imagine that—I am pretty smoking."

I nodded and put the report back in front of me and scanned it. "Let's see. It says here you were reported missing by your parents, Robert and Melinda Cobb. Your last known whereabouts was visiting your best friend Maria."

"Oh God, Maria," Raquel said. "Oh yes, I remember her."

"Oh, cool," I said, not quite sure what she meant by that. "Anyway, it looks like they called you a couple of days ago just to see how you were doing, that sort of thing. You never responded. After a day or so of trying to contact you, your parents, fearing the worst, decided to file a missing persons report. Unfortunately," I said, grabbing my briefcase from the backseat, opening it, and placing the papers in there, "It looks like their worst fears came true." Shutting the briefcase demonstrably, I tossed it back to where it once was.

71

"What do you mean?" Raquel asked. "Oh! Oh... right."

"Anyway, an address was provided with the report. It gives us a lead, at least."

"Are we headed to my parents' house, then?"

"Yes indeed," I said with conviction. I typed the address into my phone and adjusted my mirror a bit before heading to the desired destination.

"So, Raquel," I said while we were on the road. "Looking forward to seeing your parents again?"

"Yes, I guess so," she said somberly.

"Why so glum, Raquel?" I asked earnestly. "Do you have any issues with your parents?"

"No, not at all!" Raquel protested. "In fact, it couldn't be any further from the truth! I absolutely adored my parents; they were always so kind and sweet to me. They could be a little overbearing at times, that's for sure, but they always looked out for my best interests. I know they cared for me deeply and always encouraged me to do whatever I wanted in life. They truly believed I could accomplish anything."

"Then why are you hesitant to see them?"

"I'm not hesitant!" she insisted. "I mean, okay, maybe I am. But the thing is, I want to see them, but I don't. I mean, I don't want to see them like this, you know? Not as a ghost."

"I suppose I can understand that, but it's not as if they would be able to see you. You could still see them and see how they are doing."

"I guess so," she said in a tone that made me believe she was still not quite sure how to feel. My GPS made its final instruction and I turned left into the driveway of a yellow-brown vinyl sided rambler. I parked next to the white garage and looked over to my ghostly companion. "We're here," I said.

"Already? It seemed like a short trip."

"Apparently your parents don't live too far away from the police station. Anyway, let's get going."

Raquel gave me a hesitant single nod after a short, contemplative pause. I grabbed my briefcase from my backseat and exited the car, my friend following closely behind. We had arrived at the reddish-brown door when I heard a voice in my right ear.

"Vinnie," Raquel said. "I don't think I can do this."

"What do you mean?" I asked.

"I can't see my parents, it's too painful. They cared for me for so long and loved me so much. I can't bear the thought of seeing them, seeing how much they miss me, and how much they'll hope for me to arrive home safely soon, while knowing full well that they'll never…they'll never see me again."

"I've never heard this from a ghost either," I said. "But what you're saying makes sense. I'm thinking maybe you're just more empathetic and compassionate than most ghosts, Raquel, and that's why you're asking me these questions and saying all of this. You obviously don't have to follow me in. I can do this on my own."

"Shall I wait in the car? That way you know where to find me, and I'll still be close by just in case."

"Sure, sounds like a plan. I'll let you know when I'm done here."

I watched Raquel float back into my car and take her place in my passenger seat. We gave each other a thumbs up to confirm she was ready for me to continue.

With that out of the way, I approached her parents' abode. "I guess I won't be needing this right now," I muttered to myself as I pulled the Bluetooth out of my ear and put it into my front pocket.

I knocked on the mahogany door. A large, burly, raven-haired mustachioed man wearing a black turtle neck sweater and beige khaki pants greeted me. "Yes? How may I help you?"

"My name is Vincent Pietro," I said. "I've heard from Officer Ed Bergeron that you filed a police report yesterday inquiring into the whereabouts of your daughter, Raquel Cobb."

"Yes, that would be correct," the man said. "Are you with the police?"

I reached into my wallet, pulled out my private investigator license, and handed it to him. "No sir," I explained. "I'm a private investigator."

"It was my understanding that the police were going to find my daughter," he said, handing me back my license.

"Sir, the police are very busy with a large volume of cases that run the entire gamut from murder to traffic violations. They often outsource missing persons cases and other similar work to private investigators in order to lessen their work load a bit." Honestly, I had no idea whether that was true or not. I knew that nobody on the police force had actually approached me with a case, but it was my most often used excuse, and it almost always worked.

"I never actually heard of that. Is this a new thing?"

"It's been going on for several years, at least, but yes, you would be correct, this is a relatively new program." It was fun to lie.

"I appreciate your help, Vincent. God knows we'll need all the help in the world to find our little Raquel. However, I'm afraid I'm not sure if my wife and I would be able to afford your services. Money is very tight right now. We'll pay you what we can, though. Anything to get our little girl back."

"Well, that's the beauty of this arrangement, sir. Payment is actually being handled by the police force. As long as you pay your taxes, you'll be paying for my services."

"Oh really? That's good. I suppose if nothing else, it'd be good to have an extra set of eyeballs looking for her."

"Would you mind if we went inside so I can ask you a few questions?"

"Oh, yes, of course, please come in, Vincent."

With that, we entered his abode.

Yeah, I know, it's not a smart business practice to lie about payment and do the work pro bono, but that's what I did, and I stand by my decision. I already knew his daughter had died. Her spirit was literally talking to me. Somehow charging the father and mother for a search that was guaranteed to be futile seemed needlessly cruel, and would make me feel like I was taking advantage of the situation. It's one thing to lie in order to get information that could be useful towards putting a spirit to rest. It's another to profit from it. You'd have to be a real jackass to do something like that.

The man guided me into the living room where a small, brunette woman wearing a long-sleeved yellow shirt and white pants was sitting in an armchair next to an empty beige couch.

"I just realized that I haven't introduced myself to you, Vincent. My name is Robert Cobb. It is a pleasure to meet you." He extended his hand and we shook. "Honey," he said to the woman, who had risen from the armchair after our handshake. "This man is Vincent Pietro. He's a private investigator who is helping the police find our daughter."

"Oh, hello, Mr. Pietro," the woman said, shaking my hand with a much softer grip. "My name is Melinda Cobb. We appreciate your help."

"It is no problem whatsoever. Would you mind if I

sit over here and asked you a few questions?" I asked, gesturing towards the couch.

"Not at all, please do," Melinda said as she sat back into her armchair. Her husband walked behind it and placed his hands on the back of her chair as a show of emotional support. I tried to place my briefcase on the card table in the middle of the living room, but realized there were a bunch of playing cards there.

"Oh, I apologize for that," Robert said, quickly gathering the cards. "My wife and I had some friends over last night to play some Hearts. It's a weekly thing. We put this table in the middle here to give us more room to play. However, we ended the game early. Neither my wife nor I were really in the mood to play because of Raquel, of course. Apparently we didn't finish cleaning up, so I apologize for that."

"Oh no, it's no problem whatsoever," I said, as I put my briefcase on the now empty table. I opened it, pulled out my notebook, and began my questioning.

"When did you last see your daughter?" I asked.

"A few days ago—I believe it was Thursday of last week," Melinda said.

"What was the nature of the visit?"

"It was a celebration, really," Robert explained. "We had just seen her play. I believe it was called *An Officer, A Pirate, and a Princess.*"

"*A Pirate, An Officer, and a Princess,*" Melinda corrected.

"Ah yes, *A Pirate, An Officer, and a Princess*. We hadn't had a chance to see her earlier, unfortunately, due to conflicts with our schedule, but we were able to see her finale performance. She stopped by to thank us and tell us an exciting announcement."

"She had auditioned and was cast as Christine in the production of *The Phantom of the Opera* in Seattle," Melinda continued. "So we had an impromptu celebration with her. We are so proud of her for that."

"So your daughter is an actress?"

"Yes, an amazing one too," Robert said. "I know every parent feels that way about their child, but I truly believe she has a special ability to act."

"The fact that she is going to be part of a famous play in Seattle is a testament to her acting ability," I said, fighting back my melancholy as I began to realize the weight of the tragedy of my acquaintance's death. "Where did she previously act?"

"The Lakewood Townhouse," Robert said. "Small fry compared to where she'll be next."

"According to the report, the last time you saw your daughter she was headed to her friend Maria's house?"

"Yes. She told us that she was going to her friend Maria's duplex. They had planned to celebrate her new role and future in Seattle."

"Was her behavior odd at all? Did she mention anything that seemed strange or unusual to you?"

"Not really," Melinda said. "She seemed as happy

and energetic as usual. Maybe she was a little more excited because she just landed that new role of hers, of course."

"Not to mention her new man," the father said.

"Oh yes, she did mention that there was someone new in her life, didn't she?" the mother confirmed.

"New man? What new man?" I asked.

"Honestly, we don't know much about him," Melinda said. "She just mentioned someone in passing. In fact, she was actually very secretive about it, as if she had mentioned him by accident."

"It was a bit odd," the father confirmed. "The only thing she really told us about him was that he was handsome, and that she had known him for a little while, but only now she felt he was ready to express how he felt about her."

"Can you describe him for me?"

"I'm afraid not," Robert said. "We didn't even know that he existed."

"Do you know where he lives? Or where the two of them met?"

"No, sorry," Melinda said.

"Did she give you a name, at least?"

"No, I'm afraid not," Robert said.

"Hmm, interesting."

"You don't think he has anything to do with her disappearance, do you?" Melinda asked.

"I can't honestly say. Other than that he presumably

exists, nothing is known about the man."

"We understand," Melinda said. "We're just worried, that's all. She is incredibly naïve when it comes to men and relationships. You would think such a lovely girl wouldn't have trouble finding someone, but I don't think she has even dated since high school, and even then she didn't date that often."

"Perhaps we were a bit too overbearing at times," Robert said. "Regardless, we just hope this man didn't take advantage of her naivety."

"How often does your daughter visit you?" I asked.

"She generally visits us once or twice a week, so her being gone for nearly five days was a bit unusual, but nothing too worrisome. We texted her just to ask how things were going. When we didn't receive an answer we tried calling her. We called her several times and never received an answer. After a day or so of calling and receiving no answer, we visited her apartment. When she wasn't there, we filed the missing persons report."

"Do you have access to her apartment?"

"Yes, we do," Robert confirmed. "I have a spare key."

"Would you be willing to show me around? Perhaps I could find a clue that would help me out in this investigation."

"Of course," Robert said. "I'd be happy to show you around. Her apartment isn't too far away from here, perhaps a twenty-minute drive or so. Would you like to head over there now?"

"Yes, that would be great. I just have to make a quick phone call first. Would you mind if I stepped outside for a moment? I will return as soon as I am done."

"No problem at all, Vincent. Please, make your phone call."

I got up from my seat and then stepped outside, closing the door quietly behind me. Just in case anyone was around, I placed the Bluetooth in my ear and pretended to dial in some numbers on my cell phone. After a second or two, I called out, "Raquel, are you around here somewhere?" I turned to my left and looked briefly around, but could not find her. I turned completely around and looked around again, and still could not find her.

"Boo!"

"Oh, for the love of God!" I screamed. Raquel was floating right above my face, having seemingly materialized right before my eyes as I turned towards the road.

"Sorry, Vinnie! I'm sorry! I was just being silly, I didn't mean to scare you!"

"Why do you keep doing that to me?"

"I'm really sorry. I heard you calling out to me, and when I saw you looking around I just thought it'd be a fun way to get your attention, that's all. I really didn't mean to frighten you."

"It's okay," I said after having caught my breath. "Don't worry about it. I know you didn't mean it."

81

"So, how was the visit with my parents?" Raquel asked.

"Actually, that's kind of what I wanted to talk to you about. I'm not quite done with them yet. We are headed over to your apartment. I just wanted to give you a heads up in case you are still feeling uncomfortable."

"Oh, I see." After a slight hesitation, Raquel continued. "I'm sorry, Vinnie. I don't think I can do it. I still can't bear to see them."

"Okay, I understand. That's why I warned you. You can hide in my car if you'd like, maybe in my backseat. You'll see me come in, and you can follow me without ever having to see your father."

"Good idea. I think I will do that."

"Sounds like a plan."

I saw Raquel float into my backseat, and after pretending to hang up my phone and placing the Bluetooth back into my pocket, I reentered the abode.

"Okay, Robert. I'm ready to go whenever you are," I said. "Thank you for your patience."

"It's no problem, young man," he said. "Let us head out now."

I entered my car and followed Robert to Raquel's apartment. Raquel stayed in the back seat for the entire trip, hardly saying a word. We engaged in a bit of small talk, sharing a few words here or there, but it was obvious that the stress of the situation was overwhelming to my ghostly companion, so I decided to not press the issue particularly hard. It was, for the most part, an uncomfortably silent trip. I had grown accustomed to our long conversations.

Robert parked in the main lot near the entrance of the three story, brick and yellow vinyl-sided apartment complex. I stopped by his car and he pointed me over to the visitor lot on the western side of the facility. "The Coldstone Apartments," I muttered to myself as I passed by the sign into the visitors' lot.

After pulling my car into an open spot, I joined Robert at the entrance and we entered the facility. Though I was mesmerized momentarily with an aquarium in the lobby, Robert was able to snap me out of my daze as we walked through the lavender hallway to the stairwell.

We went up the stairs and went to room eighteen. After Robert had unlocked the door, we both entered the room, walking on the parquet flooring, and began our search for clues. In the middle of the living room was a television, a coffee table, a couch, and a sofa. Two things were on the coffee table—a set of playing cards and a group of papers tied together with three silver rings. I picked up the set of playing cards and said to Robert, "It looks like your daughter is also into card games."

"Yes indeed. I believe her favorite game is Commune, of all games."

"I never even heard of it."

"You should try it sometime. It's a fun game."

I nodded slightly and placed the cards back on the

83

table. My attention turned to the stack of papers. The words *A Pirate, An Officer, and a Princess* were emblazoned on the front. I picked them up and wiped off the layer of dust that had gathered on the cover. I skimmed through the sheets of paper, and it became quite obvious that it was the script to the play Raquel was in.

"I believe this is your daughter's script," I said to Robert. "Would you mind if I took it?"

"No, I suppose that would be all right, if you would think it would help you with your case."

"I'm not sure if it will, but since it is a play your daughter was part of, it could come in handy," I explained. The father gave me a slight nod and I slipped the script into my briefcase.

The rest of the room didn't have anything particularly notable. There were some shoes in the corner near the entrance, some glass trinkets and other assorted items on her mantle, and a few remnants of what I assumed to be costumes lying on the couch, but nothing too unusual or significant.

I noticed a large manual on the kitchen counter. Taking a closer look at it, I realized that it was a manual for self-defense with a firearm. "Was your daughter an avid gunman?" I asked Robert.

"I actually insisted on that," explained the man. "I got my daughter a gun and had her take lessons over at the local gun range in order to defend herself. She's an attractive young girl living alone. She needs something to protect her."

I nodded in agreement and placed the manual back down on the table.

Other than the firearm manual, the combination kitchen and dining room did not show any signs of abnormal activity, or anything else particularly out of the ordinary. Assorted kitchen ware was where you'd expect it to be. Maybe a fork or two was not put away and some dishes were still in the sink, but otherwise I didn't see anything particularly unusual, except for one particular item.

The rotting fruit on the kitchen table was a notable thing, as it suggested that she had not been there for a few days—something I knew already, naturally. I had been speaking to Raquel's spirit after all. Robert didn't know that I already knew that, though, so I pretended otherwise when I pointed out the fruit to Robert. He merely gave me a somber sigh in return. He knew it wasn't a good sign.

After taking a quick look around, we entered her bedroom. In the middle of the room was a queen-sized bed with a tie-dyed, rainbow colored comforter with lily white pillows lying on top of it. At the foot of the bed was a small, tablet like device. I picked it up and realized that it was a Kindle. After waking up the device, I saw that the current passage read:

Then we noticed that in the second pillow was the indentation of a head. One of us lifted something from it, and leaning forward, that faint and invisible dust dry and acrid to the nostrils, we saw a long strand of iron-gray hair.

After playing around a bit on the electronic apparatus, I learned that Raquel was reading a collection of assorted short stories by William Faulkner. The current story was entitled "A Rose for Emily." I glanced around the room a bit, and noticed to the left of her bed was a bookshelf, tall enough to almost touch the ceiling and filled with all sorts of books, most notably various novels and compilations of short stories. Apparently, Raquel was a big fan of those kinds of works.

"Raquel loves to read," Robert said, pointing at his daughter's Kindle still in my hand, "She takes after me in that respect. A lot of these books were originally mine. The Kindle was a birthday gift that we gave her in May."

I nodded to acknowledge the man's statement. I sighed and rubbed the back of my neck as I put down the Kindle and looked around, and noticed a shelf full of stuffed animals to the right of her bed.

It took me a second, but soon I realized I actually recognized some of the characters on the shelf. Hamster Runner, Sad Tree Pals, even Tyco of Tyco's Elementary School fame? I hadn't even thought of that one in years. I didn't recognize all of the characters, but I recognized enough to know that all of the toys were characters of various web animated series.

"Is your daughter a big fan of web animation, Robert?"

"Web animation? What do you mean by that?"

"I suppose the best way to describe it is Internet cartoons."

"No, I don't believe she is a particular fan of them. Oh wait, are you referring to the shelf over there?" Robert asked, pointing at the shelf full of stuffed animals.

"Yes I am."

"Oh, she doesn't have them because she's a fan. She has them because she has done voice acting for a lot of Internet cartoons. They sent her those stuffed animals to show their appreciation. Apparently, she is very popular online—at least, that's what she told us. I am completely unfamiliar with Internet cartoons."

I picked up the plushy of Hamster Runner. "I'm kind of a closet fan, to be honest with you, and I actually know of a couple of these characters. I'll be honest, though—I don't recall ever hearing the name Raquel Cobb."

"Maybe my daughter was exaggerating her popularity, then."

"Not necessarily. Do you know your daughter's screen name?"

"What do you mean by screen name? I know what a screen name is generally, but why would that be interesting to you?"

"Many voice actors and actresses use a pseudonym of sorts—or perhaps it would be better described as a stage name—when doing cartoons online. Most people don't want the Internet at large to know their real name, for various reasons."

"Ah, that makes sense. Now that you mention it, I think my daughter mentioned something about being called Raquel Weasel, or something like that?"

"Raquel Weevil? Your daughter is Raquel Weevil?"

"Yes, Weevil. That's right, Raquel Weevil. Have you heard of her?"

"Heard of her? She's great! She is pretty famous in Internet circles. I remember watching one cartoon and thinking there were five different voice actresses, and was stunned when I found out Raquel Weevil did all of them."

"She's also excellent at impressions. You should hear her sometime. She imitates her mother perfectly, as well as her friend Maria. It is hilarious and remarkable all at the same time. She can even imitate Taylor Swift pretty well. She really does have a lot of talent, Vincent."

"Wow. It's true, you learn something new every day," I said, as I placed Hamster Runner back in his original place.

"I'm sure Raquel would be more than happy to give you an autograph when we find her," Robert said with a weak chuckle. I smiled weakly in response.

I took one last long look in the room and motioned to Robert that I wanted to head back out. He nodded and followed me out.

"Did you find anything that could help you, Mr. Pietro?" Robert asked, as I headed towards the door.

"All of this information was interesting and gave me a better picture of what kind of person Raquel is, but unfortunately, I didn't learn anything that could lead to her whereabouts," I said. "I guess the only thing I can do now is find out if her friends know any more than we do. You mentioned that she had a friend named Maria. Would you happen to know where she lives?"

"Yes, my daughter told me she lives in The Whetstone Duplexes over on Main Street. I forget specifically what apartment number, though."

"It's okay. I'm sure I can find it listed somewhere, or at least find someone there who can help me out. You wouldn't happen to know her last name, would you? If I know that, I could probably look her up in a directory when I'm there."

"Richardson. Maria Richardson. We were actually planning on visiting her ourselves, my wife and I, but after filing the missing persons report we assumed that the officer in charge would be visiting her himself. The fact that he hasn't yet is awfully disappointing. Having said that, I'm glad you've arrived and offered your assistance."

"Thank you very much, Robert. You have been a big help."

"Please keep me informed, Vincent. Our daughter is our entire world. We need to know she's safe."

I swallowed hard and sighed softly as I said, "Of course, Robert. Please give me your phone number so

89

I can keep you up to date with whatever I find." We exchanged numbers and a hearty handshake. I turned around and headed towards my car.

I entered my car, and after placing my phone in the charger and tossing my briefcase in the backseat, I began looking up the address for The Whetstone. Suddenly, I felt a second pair of eyes hovering over my phone.

"Hello, Raquel," I said. Raquel was next to me, looking at my lap where I had placed the phone. "I see you've moved from the back seat to the front."

"My father is gone, right?" she asked.

"Yes he is," I confirmed.

"Did you find anything that helps us with our case?"

"Not particularly. At least, no solid leads or clues so far. I did learn something, though."

"What's that?"

"It sounds to me like you were quite the actress," I said to Raquel.

"Actress. Imagine that. The word 'actress' is starting to jog some memories for me, Vinnie."

"See, I told you you'd start remembering things once we started finding out things about your past."

"You're right," Raquel said. "Wow, it really is like a wave." After marveling over her recovered memories for a moment, my ghostly friend continued, "I was the best. I was destined for Hollywood. I'm sure of it."

"Sounds like it."

"I really loved acting, Vinnie. I even loved being part

of *A Pirate, An Officer, and a Princess,* even though it was only a play at a smalltime theater. I only left because I needed to move on to better things."

"I have to know, what is the play about? *A Pirate, An Officer, and a Princess?*"

"Oh, you've never seen the play?"

"I've never even heard of it," I confessed. "I have your script in my briefcase. I was going to read it if there was any free time."

"It's a wonderful play, and incredibly funny as well! It's a love triangle about a princess of an island nation who wins the attention of a British officer and a local pirate. The British officer is after the local pirate, thinking he is up to no good and terrorizing the islanders, when in reality the pirate is helping them all out. It's a farce in a similar vein to an Oscar Wilde play, but I still loved it. I would have changed the ending, though."

"What's wrong with the ending?"

"She winds up with the pirate and spurns the officer."

"The ending is too predictable for your liking, I assume."

"Well, I suppose there's that, but it's more that the officer was such a wonderful man. He was smart and funny. He was bound by duty, willing to help out others and do what was right even if it didn't directly benefit him. He may have been mistaken about the pirate's motivations, but that doesn't mean that he wasn't doing his best to do good in the world. He never even asked for a reward for his efforts, and wound up helping the pirate confess his love for the princess when he realized the two of them were in love with each other. Imagine that—he loved the princess, but let someone else have her.

"Now, we were all supposed to laugh at him. Critics said he was a little over the top with his emotions, and that he fell for the princess way too quickly. They also didn't like him because he tried to impress the princess with his vast intellect, which made them think he was arrogant. I don't know if I agree, though. I always found him sincere. Near the end of the play he sings a song about how even though he loved her, since the pirate and the princess were in love with each other, it was his duty to bring them together. It was the duty of an officer to aid others, even if it ultimately wound up hurting him. He had a bit of a temper and was a bit overzealous at times, but he was overall a really good man. I always thought the princess should have wound up with him. Of course, nobody ever actually knew I felt this way. I don't mean to brag, but I really was a great actress."

"You make the play actually sound pretty good. With that dopey title I thought the play would be pretty lame, but you make it sound fun. I'll have to watch it sometime." I scratched my head and let my mind wander a bit, thinking about the Kindle and her collection of short stories, and even an earlier conversation between the two of us.

"By the way," I said, after a short pause. "Have you

ever read the short story, 'You Can't Just Walk On By'?"

"I can't say I have. But then again, it's hard to remember with this 'Swiss cheese' memory, as you call it," Raquel said, putting air quotes around "Swiss cheese." "Why do you ask?"

"It's just that I saw your Kindle full of short stories by William Faulkner, and your collection of short stories on your bookshelf. You must have loved to read."

"I believe I did. I believe I loved all sorts of stories, not just short stories, Vinnie. I remember loving all the classic writers such Faulkner, C.S. Lewis, Robert Browning, and Stephen King. You know, authors like them."

"It sounds to me like you liked a whole smorgasbord of authors." She giggled in response as I continued. "I just thought you might have come across the story I mentioned sometime in your life."

"If I have, I certainly don't remember it now."

"That's okay. It's just a short story written by Borden Deal that I read in middle school. When the author was a child, he saw a water moccasin, a pretty nasty poisonous snake. Now, he knew he could avoid the snake altogether. He saw it, he knew the danger, and he knew how to avoid the danger. But if he did that, somebody else was at risk—somebody less experienced and far less likely to notice the snake. And even if they did, they may not grasp the inherent danger. Because of this, he decided to kill the snake and succeeded, but nearly died doing so.

"The story concludes with him having a better

appreciation of life after his near-death experience, but I always thought the very idea of helping others for the sake of helping others was inspiring. Nobody would ever know that he was the one that killed the water moccasin and saved other people's lives. He just did it because he was there and saw the potential threat, and could do something about it. Hence the title, 'You Just Can't Walk On By.'"

"Is that your favorite story, Vinnie?"

"I suppose it is."

"Vinnie?" Raquel asked, after a short moment of silence between the two of us. "Is that why you help out ghosts?"

"Yes, Raquel, I think that is the reason."

"You really are a good man, Vinnie."

"Thank you. It's about time somebody recognized that." I smiled broadly at my companion. "Now, I suppose we should go and visit Maria," I said as I started the car and we headed to our next destination.

CHAPTER 4

"Oh God, Maria, I can't wait to visit her," Raquel said, rolling her eyes as we drove to Maria's place. At least, she rolled her eyes as well as she could reasonably be expected to, considering blood seemed to be constantly streaming down them.

"Are you looking forward to seeing your best friend?" I asked.

"Best friend," Raquel scoffed. "She wasn't my best friend."

"Really? But then, why did the report and your parents say that Maria was your best friend? Your parents said the two of you were really close."

"Appearances can be deceiving," Raquel said. "Don't get me wrong. Maria is a nice enough girl. There's nothing particularly wrong with her. We treated each other well and we had some good times together. She was just too much of a ditz for my tastes."

"What do you mean by that?"

"She just wasn't that smart, and the way she spoke drove me insane. Here, I'll do an impression of her really quickly, so that you can hear what I mean." She paused for a second, before saying, in a much higher pitched, shrill voice, "Like, oh my God, Raquel. You would totally not believe who I saw checking you out at the mall today, girl. It was that total hotty Vinnie. Like, he is so cute! You should totally go out with him, girl!"

I chuckled. "Is that really what she sounds like?"

"I might have exaggerated how much of a valley girl she is, if I'm honest," Raquel said, returning to her more normal voice. "But I think I have the voice down pretty well."

"I'm going to have to take your word for it, at least until I actually meet the girl in question."

"Trust me. It is a very accurate imitation."

"No bias whatsoever in that evaluation, I'm sure," I said, smirking.

"Maybe a little bit of bias," she said, moving her index finger and thumb close together while smiling. "But regardless, you get the idea. It's so annoying. She's almost twenty-one years old, and she sounds like a thirteen-year-old. I just want her to act her age, that's all."

"That makes sense. Not everyone can be as mature as you, though, so I wouldn't judge her too harshly."

"You have a point."

"I have to say, your father told me that you were an incredible impressionist, so biased or not, I wouldn't be surprised if you were dead on. I still can't believe you were Raquel Weevil!"

"Oh, did my father tell you about that?"

"Yeah, after I saw your plushy of Hamster Runner."

"I can't believe you even heard of me."

"Are you kidding? You were the best! As I said to your father, I was shocked when I found out you were the voice of all the women characters in the cartoon Hamster Runner. It must have been a lot of work for you to disguise your voice so well."

"Strangely, no. Voice acting and imitations come naturally for me for some reason. I suppose it was a gift."

"For some it may be a gift. For others, a curse. Does it truly matter? We all have our crosses to bear."

"Wow, Vinnie."

"Did you like that?"

"Yeah, it was almost deep and meaningful."

"Hey," I said, raising my index finger sarcastically towards the girl, barely able to suppress my smile. "Never question the Tao of Vincent Pietro."

"Okay, okay," she replied, raising her hands, holding her palms out in a mocking gesture. "I will never question you, Mr. Guru of Wisdom."

We both laughed and continued our playful banter until we arrived at Maria's duplex, The Whetstone.

After parallel parking across from it, we walked across the street and entered the facility. I checked the directory and ascertained that she lived in room number twenty-one. That room was on the second floor, and a relatively short walk from the stairwell. We walked through the burgundy hallway and up the stairs, and when we reached our destination, I gave the door an earth-rattling knock.

From behind the door I heard a low, incoherent discussion, and while I was still processing what was said, I heard a couple of bolts unlatch and the lock open. I was greeted by a young woman with long, flowing auburn hair, a thin body, and piercing blue eyes peering through a pair of thick, black-rimmed glasses. She wore blue jeans and a sweater that had all sorts of writing and a couple of childlike drawings on it.

"Hello," she said. "Can I help you?"

Raquel's impression was completely off, I thought to myself. A fantastic voice actress, perhaps, but a lousy impressionist. Both her father and the girl herself must have overrated her abilities on that front.

"Hello. My name is Vincent Pietro. I am a private investigator working with the police. Am I safe in assuming you are Maria Richardson?"

"No, I'm not. I just answered the door because Maria is — well, indisposed for a moment. She'll be here in a second. Shit, Maria already called for a private investigator?"

"Maria didn't call me. I'm here as part of an investigation of Raquel Cobb."

"What do you mean? What did Raquel do?"

"I'm not here because of anything she did. I'm here because Raquel's parents filed a missing persons report on her, and I'm investigating her disappearance."

"Holy shit, so Raquel's gone missing too?"

"Missing too? What do you mean, missing too?"

Before I could answer, I heard a flush from within the apartment. "It sounds like Maria will be here in a moment. I'll let her talk to you when she's ready. In the meantime, would you mind showing me a badge or something Mister...Pietro, was it? Or please show me an ID card, or whatever it is you private investigators have."

"Of course," I said, putting down my briefcase and fishing into my wallet. "Here you go." I handed her my private investigator license.

She looked over the card. "Thanks. I'll assume that this license is legit. I've never actually seen a private investigator's license before, so I'm going to have to take your word for it. At least you have one. My name is Elizabeth, by the way. Elizabeth Murphy."

I heard a familiar voice shout, "Thank you, Liz!"

I glanced over my right shoulder towards Raquel. "Did you say something?" I thought it was an odd time for her to start doing impressions again.

"Oh no, that was just Maria," Elizabeth said. She turned sideways towards the house. "Maria! A private investigator wants to talk to you!"

"Okay, just a second."

I quickly realized that the high-pitched shrill voice was

99

not coming from Raquel, but was instead coming from within the house. While she waited, Elizabeth smiled at me nervously, her right hand placed horizontally on one side of the doorway, my license still in that hand, and her left hand aligned over her head and placed on the other side of the doorway. Eventually she removed both hands from the door as she moved towards the right. A tall girl with shoulder length brown hair and tan skin appeared next to Elizabeth.

"This gentleman," Elizabeth said, showing the girl my license before handing it back to me, "Is a private investigator. His name is Vincent Pietro."

"Oh, hi," said the tan, brown haired girl wearing a pink sweatshirt and black pants. "So, um, what exactly are you doing here?"

"Uh, yes," I said. "Are you Maria Richardson?"

"I am. Why?"

"I'm here to talk to you on behalf of Melinda and Robert Cobb. They filed a missing persons report on Raquel a few days ago, and the last they heard from her she was visiting you, Maria."

"I love it when you use that authoritarian voice," Raquel said, giggling. I flashed a quick smile before returning to my solemn expression.

"Shut up!" Maria exclaimed. "Raquel is missing too? Like, oh my God, it just keeps getting worse and worse, doesn't it?"

"I'm afraid I'm not following," I confessed.

100

"You better come in, Mr. Pietro," Elizabeth said.

"Please, call me Vincent."

"Okay, Vincent. You better come in so we can discuss this matter further. I'm afraid we have a lot to talk about."

I followed the two women past the kitchen and dining room combination area into the living room. As per usual, Raquel followed me floating just above my right shoulder.

"Like, I just can't believe it," Maria said, as she seated herself on her beige couch in the middle of the living room, "First I lose my phone, then I learn that like, my aunt broke her neck and is in like, really bad shape and everything, then Frankie's gone missing, and then, like, Raquel too. I'm just like, so worried right now."

Before taking my seat on one of the white easy chairs placed to the left of the couch, I shared a quick glance with my ghostly companion and noticed she was wearing a broad, confirming smile as she nodded knowingly. I mouthed a quick, "You really are good!" that was fortunately not noticed by either Elizabeth nor Maria.

Elizabeth took a seat in the turquoise arm chair placed to the right of the couch. I tried to place the briefcase on the coffee table, but noticed a bunch of playing cards adorned the surface.

"Oh, sorry about that," Maria said. "Elizabeth and I were like, playing Uno to try to like, keep our minds off things. It like, didn't work. I like, haven't really had a chance to clean up yet, so please let me gather the cards real quick."

"Don't worry about it," I said, placing my briefcase next to my seat. "I can just set it here."

Maria ignored me, and gathered the cards and put them on the corner of the coffee table. With a sigh, I took out my notebook once again and took notes as I talked to the young ladies in front of me.

"This really is a nice place, Ms. Richardson," I said to open the conversation.

"Please call me Maria, and thank you very much."

"Let's start from the top. Maria, you just said that a gentleman named Frankie is missing. Who is Frankie?"

"Frankie is my boyfriend," Maria said. "We've been dating since we were like, seniors in high school."

"He's also my brother," Elizabeth said. "His full name is Franklyn Murphy."

"How long has he been missing?"

"I'm not quite sure, to be honest. Like, I only found out he was missing today, but he may have been gone like, since a few days ago."

"What do you mean?"

"I lost my cell phone like, a couple of days ago, so I'm not like, quite sure how long he may have been missing."

"I'm sorry," I said, rubbing the back of my neck with my hand. "I'm a little confused right now. I'm afraid I'm not following at all."

"It's all right, Vincent," Elizabeth assured me. "It's

102

a long story. Maria, maybe you should start from the beginning."

"Okay. So like, my boyfriend Frankie went on like, a hunting trip with his uncle a few days ago," Maria began.

"About five days ago, to be exact," said Elizabeth.

"Where did he go hunting?" I asked.

"Over at my family's cabin," Elizabeth said.

"Cabin? What cabin?" I asked.

"It's my grandfather's cabin. He built it years ago over in Evergreen. It's just north of Marysville. It's in an isolated part of the woods away from civilization. Granddad built it mostly as his place to get away from the city and go hunting, that sort of thing. Everyone in the family has access to that place."

"Frankie got like, a week off of work in order to go hunting with my uncle, and he like, doesn't have to act because his play had its last show of the year like, a couple of days ago or so," Maria explained.

"Oh, so Franklyn's an actor?" I asked.

"Yeah, that's right," Elizabeth explained. "He's actually part of the same play Raquel is involved in at the Lakewood Playhouse."

"*A Pirate, An Officer, and a Princess,*" I said in confirmation.

"Oh, so you're familiar with it?" Elizabeth asked.

"I heard about it from Raquel's parents."

"You should watch it sometime. It's actually surprisingly good, better than it has any right to be. It attempts to emulate Oscar Wilde, and mostly succeeds."

"I actually have a copy of the script in my briefcase."

"So ANYWAY!" Maria screamed, interrupting our conversation. "So like, the day he left was the same day that I invited Raquel to come over to like, celebrate her successful audition with *The Phantom of the Opera* or something. She now is part of a big play with a big role, and I am like, so happy for her! That's why I had to celebrate right away! But in the middle of the celebration I wanted to like, check my messages on the cell phone in case Frankie or somebody had called me, as unlikely as it was for him to have like, called me, when I like realized my cell phone was missing! Raquel tried to help me but we like, couldn't find it!"

"So you've been missing your cell phone and haven't been able to communicate with Franklyn in a few days, then?" I asked.

"Well, even though I've been like missing my cell phone for a couple of days now, it's not like I could have called him anyway. His uncle has this like, stupid 'no cell phone' rule, so he couldn't have called me and I couldn't like, call him in the last few days anyway."

"My uncle is a big outdoorsman," Elizabeth explained. "Whenever he goes hunting with one of the members of his family, he makes them put their cell phone in this box, and the person isn't allowed to retrieve it until the hunting trip is over. I don't know, it's some sort of connecting with nature thing. I never understood it myself."

"Still, if you're missing a cell phone, wouldn't it be prudent to find a replacement?" I asked.

"I'm not like, sure what prudent means, but the reason I didn't like, replace my cell phone right away is because I knew Frankie couldn't like, text me or call me, and I couldn't like, text him or call him anyway, and I had all these like, family problems to deal with so I didn't feel like a cell phone was that important right now," Maria said.

"Family problems?" I asked. "I don't mean to pry, but what sort of family problems have you been dealing with?"

"My aunt is like, in really bad shape."

"What happened to your aunt?"

"I believe a couple of weeks ago my aunt was vacationing in like, a resort, and she like, was having boogie board lessons. I'm not sure what exactly happened, but I know she like, slipped and landed wrong and broke her neck."

"Oh my God," I said. "I'm sorry to hear that. Is she going to be all right?"

"The doctors are not sure right now. It's like, fifty-fifty or something. My family has really needed me, so I've spent most of my time like, traveling back and forth, visiting family and stuff. I haven't had like, a lot of time to myself lately, and since I thought Frankie was like, having fun killing things with his uncle, I didn't think

105

that a cell phone was that necessary."

"Wait a second. You said you 'thought' he was having fun with his uncle. Did he not go hunting with his uncle? What did you mean by that?"

"Like Maria said, we thought he was hunting with my uncle over in Evergreen," Elizabeth explained. "He was supposed to be home by this morning. I texted him a couple of times, asking him how his trip went and whether he'd given more thought to that conversation we had last weekend. He never answered me. I was a bit worried, so I gave my uncle a call asking how the trip went and how my brother was doing. He then told me a bombshell. Apparently, my uncle's girlfriend had invited him on a last second trip to Las Vegas. He had to cancel the hunting trip. My uncle had no idea why Franklyn didn't tell me or my parents this, but then assured me that he is certain that Franklyn would at least have told his girlfriend, Maria. Naturally, I then tried contacting Maria, but she didn't answer my calls or my texts either. Obviously, I know why she didn't now, but I didn't know why at the time. I just happened to be doing some shopping in the area, so I thought I'd drop by to see if she knew what was going on. That's when she told me about her missing cell phone, and how Franklyn did not tell her that the trip was cancelled."

"Of course he couldn't have told her," I said, "Because she was missing her cell phone."

"Yeah, but you'd think he'd at least visit her and tell

106

her about the trip being cancelled if he couldn't get a hold of her, or even text me or call me and tell me he was having problems contacting her and would like my help. I am always his go to girl whenever he has a problem he can't solve, which is frankly quite often."

"I see. That makes sense. So you haven't actually filed a missing persons report yet."

"Not yet. Maria and I were debating whether we should when you arrived. We were actually talking about it over a game of Uno—as Maria said earlier, and you no doubt saw when you tried to place your briefcase down on the coffee table—to calm our nerves a bit—though honestly, it didn't really work because we couldn't really concentrate on the game—when we heard your knock on the door."

"I was like, so looking forward to seeing Frankie today," Maria said. "And I was so looking forward to like, Frankie's and my anniversary this Saturday too. I thought it'd be the perfect break from all of the stress I'm under, because of like, my aunt and everything."

"It's funny," Elizabeth said. "You can forget his birthday, my birthday, your parent's birthday—hell, even your own birthday—but you seem to never forget your anniversary."

"Hey, that's not true!"

"When's my birthday, then? Or how about Frankie's birthday, huh?"

"Your birthday is like…um…well, at least Frankie's

birthday is in like, June or something, right...?"

"August," Elizabeth said.

"Okay, but I've never like, forgotten my own birthday! And our anniversary is a day I could like, never possibly forget!"

"How very romantic." Elizabeth's words dripped with sarcasm.

"Anyway, right now all I like, really want to know is whether Frankie is like, okay or not." After a reflective pause, Maria continued, "On top of all of this, Raquel has like, gone missing too?"

"I'm afraid so," I said. "The report was filed by her parents yesterday."

"God, that's awful," Elizabeth said.

"What was your relationship with Raquel, Maria?" I asked.

"Relationship? What do you mean by relationship? Oh, wait, you mean like, how did we know each other and stuff like that?"

"Yes," I said with a sigh. "That's what I meant."

"Oh, sorry. She's like, only my best friend in the world. Liz didn't really like her, though."

"I never said I didn't like her. All I said was I really didn't really know her. I respected the hell out of her, though. She's one hell of an actress."

"How long have you known Raquel, Maria?"

"Raquel and I have been like, best friends since high school. The two of us met when we were like, freshmen.

We were part of the drama club. We like, did plays together and stuff."

"So the two of you have been close ever since your freshman year in high school."

"Not exactly," Maria said. "It's funny. We knew each other when we were like, freshmen, but we didn't really become that close until we were like, seniors. She started talking to me more then, and like, we started doing things together more and more after school."

"The two of you knew each other since freshmen year, but didn't become friends until your senior year?"

"I know! It's kind of like, we knew of each other, but really didn't know each other. I actually kind of like, thought she didn't really like me or anything, she always seemed so cold. It turned out she was like, actually very nice, and just shy."

"She never seemed shy to me," commented Elizabeth. She shrugged as she said, "But then again, appearances can be deceiving. It may be because she has such a strong stage presence that I just assumed she was very extroverted outside of acting. Sometimes the best actors are actually very shy. Rowan Atkinson is actually very shy in public. You wouldn't know that by the way he acts."

"Rowan Atkinson?"

"He's done a ton of comedic roles like *Blackadder, The Thin Blue Line, Johnny English*. But you probably know him best as *Mr. Bean*."

109

"Oh, yeah, *Mr. Bean*. I like that guy."

"A lot of people become different when they are on stage. Even my brother is completely different than the character he plays. He's much more aloof and irresponsible. He also doesn't have the dry wit that his character does. He has a sense of humor, sure, but he's mostly a prankster. Definitely thinks he's funnier than he is. Besides, to think my brother would have the grades to be an officer at any time period is a bit of a laugh. He struggled every year with his remedial classes to keep his grades up to make the football team. "And frankly," she said, moving closer to me, "He's much more selfish. Not towards you, Maria," Elizabeth said, turning towards Maria, a statement that elicited a wide smile from the young lady. "All his faults aside, he does put her first. But other than Maria he always puts himself first. Plus, he just can't let things go. He still wears his letterman jacket around. It's been three years since he's played, it's been two years since he graduated. It's time to move on, wouldn't you agree?"

"Yes, of course. He needs to let things go," I said hesitatingly, not admitting that I had only stopped wearing my letterman's jacket a year ago, and even then only because I got a tear in the left elbow.

"I think he looks dreamy in that jacket," swooned Maria.

"Of course you do," Elizabeth sighed. "Of course you do."

"Moving on," I said. "Elizabeth. How long have you known Raquel?"

"I actually haven't known her for very long. I've only talked to her a couple of times when I visited Maria and she happened to be there. In fact, I didn't even know of her until my brother began acting with her at the Lakewood Playhouse. Maria, on the other hand, I met through my brother Franklyn. The two of them began dating—what was it, your senior year in high school?"

"Yep!" Maria confirmed.

"Yeah, I was a sophomore at the University of Washington, Tacoma at the time. I'm graduating this June, in case you were wondering, though honestly, I'm not sure why you'd be wondering."

"Always good to get a time frame," I chuckled.

"I had like, the biggest crush on him before that, though," Maria said gushingly. "He was a member of the football team, and he was like, so hot and everything. But I didn't actually meet him until he was like, part of the play!"

"Drama club teacher saw his build and thought he'd be perfect for the role of Boo Radley in the school production of *To Kill a Mockingbird*," Elizabeth explained. "I don't know—that teacher was weird, and took, shall we say, a few liberties with the original story."

"I liked it! I thought it was fun!"

"Yes, I know," Elizabeth sighed. "My brother figured why the hell not. He'd busted his knee his junior year

111

and couldn't play football anymore, so he decided to take the role. That's where my brother caught the acting bug. He actually did a pretty decent job, too—we were all surprised that he could actually act. Obviously, he stuck with the drama club for the rest of the year, and as you can guess, he still hasn't quite kicked the habit yet."

"Frankie's like, going to be a star one day!" Maria said excitedly.

"I don't know about that," Elizabeth said. "Don't get me wrong. Franklyn's okay for what he is; an actor in a small local theater, a step above what you might find in high school, but nothing special. I mean, I'm glad my brother enjoys acting, but I honestly hope he keeps it up as a hobby rather than having any delusions of grandeur.

"Raquel, though—man, she absolutely dwarfs his ability. She emotes well, her line delivery is fluid and confident. For lack of a better term, she becomes the character. She's an excellent singer, too—mesmerizing, in fact. I mean, think about it. Maria told me today that she's going to be in *The Phantom of the Opera* at the Paramount Theater in Seattle, starring as Christine. She's destined for bigger and better things, Vincent."

"It sounds like you are a big fan of the theater, Elizabeth."

"Well, I mean, take a look at my shirt," she said, pointing at her sweatshirt at the same time.

"I'm afraid I'm not familiar with the reference."

"It's from *Hamilton: The Musical*. I saw it when they

had a show in Seattle. It's kind of silly, but I'm a big fan all the same."

"Wow. It seems like you really know your stuff when it comes to the theater."

"It comes with the territory. I work on the school website, specifically on articles related to the theater and the arts. I've actually been doing that kind of thing since high school. Anyway, it's my job to critique talent, so believe me when I say she is incredible."

"Frankie's a great actor, Elizabeth! He should be in Phantom too!"

"Look, Maria, Franklyn's my brother and I love him. I also admit that he's better than I'd ever thought a meathead like him would ever be. But honestly, he isn't anything special. He's strictly a community theater kind of guy. I mean, he's not even the lead in the play."

"But he looks so hot in his military uniform," Maria said.

"He's not the lead?" I asked.

"Nah, he's the officer," Elizabeth explained. "The pirate and the princess are the leads. Don't get me wrong, it's not like it's a bad role. He gets second billing, and that's pretty good. I'm just saying that's why he isn't anything special. He isn't even a big fish in a small pond."

"Are Franklyn and Raquel good friends?"

"I think they get along all right, but they aren't especially close. At least my brother has never really talked about her to me. Maria, do you know if the two of them hang out a lot?"

"I don't think so," Maria said. "I mean like, I think they do a lot of rehearsing together and stuff, but they aren't really like, that close, you know?"

"Just to confirm, Maria—the last time you saw her was after your little get together, your celebration?"

"Yep. We drank some wine and played cards and stuff like that. When I wanted to like, check my cell phone to see if I had any messages or something, I found out it was missing. Raquel like, tried to help me find it, but it started to get late and I had to like, visit my family because of my aunt thing, you know? I told her we would find it later, and she said like, 'okay,' and then told me she was like, headed home. That's like, pretty much all I know."

"Was she acting weird in any way? Did she tell you where she might have been going? Is there anything she might have said that seemed unusual to you? Did she seem troubled at all? Depressed? Upset?"

"Not really," said Maria. "I mean, she was like, talking mostly about how she had big plans and how things were going to like, change and everything. I assumed she was like, just excited about her new role, that's all."

"That's a pretty safe assumption," Elizabeth said. "It's like one of those bets where if you bet a dollar and win you'd only get fifty cents back."

"If anything, Raquel was like, happier than usual."

I began to look over my notes a little bit. Something

that Maria just said jogged something in my memory. Something I had forgotten about. Something her parents had told me.

"Oh, that's right," I said upon reading a familiar scribble. "I had forgotten about this until just now. Did Raquel mention anything about a new man in her life? Her parents told me that Raquel had talked to them about a new man, but was very secretive about it. I was wondering if she shared that information with you two."

"Shut up! Raquel has a man?" Maria shrieked. "I didn't know that! How about you, Liz? Did she like, tell you about her man?"

"It's the first I heard about it," Elizabeth mused, but then shrugged her shoulders and said, "But like I said, the two of us aren't very close."

"Why wouldn't she tell me, though?" Maria asked. "I'm like, her best friend."

"That's...," Elizabeth said. "That's actually an excellent question."

"Ladies," I said, closing my notebook. "I thank you both for your time. Our conversation together was very informative. I'm sure this information will be very helpful in finding her."

In truth, the conversation, though enlightening in many ways, didn't actually provide much as far as leads were concerned. I was honestly a bit flummoxed. Still, it wasn't like I was going to confess that to the two ladies in front of me. A private investigator has to keep up

115

appearances.

"Please tell me when you find her," Maria said. "She's like, my best friend after all. I need to know, like, if she is safe or not. So much is happening right now with Frankie gone and my aunt being hurt and everything, I need to like, know she's okay, at least."

"Yes, please let me know as well," Elizabeth said.

"Of course," I said. "Thank you both once again. Have a great rest of your day." With that, I waved and the motion was reciprocated by the two ladies.

As I headed out the door, I overheard Maria say, "Liz? Would you mind helping me like, look for my phone? Maybe Frankie left me like, a message or something and I missed it. I think it's still around the house. It's an Android phone, and its cover is like, pink with a white flower-like design on the back."

"I'm afraid I don't have time right now, Maria. I have something to do. Don't worry, I'll be back."

I heard Maria's whine of "Okay" a moment before I shut the door behind me.

I had not walked even two steps towards my car before I heard the door open behind me and a familiar voice say, "Mr. Pietro? Would you mind if I pulled you aside for a moment to talk to you privately?"

I turned around. "Not at all, Elizabeth. What seems to be on your mind?"

"As you could probably tell, I'm very worried about my brother," Elizabeth said.

"Yeah, it's pretty obvious, and also understandable."

"Anyway, I was thinking that, since you're here — and I know you're not exactly a police officer, but you're pretty close — I was wondering whether you would mind helping us out a bit."

"I wouldn't say that I'm pretty close to a police officer, if I'm being honest now."

"You know what I mean. You probably have a better eye for this kind of thing than I do anyway. Plus, if nothing else, it's good to get some help from someone who is experienced with investigating."

"I don't know. My focus should really be on finding Raquel."

"Please, Vincent, I'm begging you. I am willing to pay you anything."

I couldn't help but think of a couple of movies I'd seen that started that way, but quickly dismissed any ungentlemanly thoughts.

I knew I should have rejected her outright, but when a person comes to me asking for something so sincerely, it is nearly impossible for me to deny such a request. Besides, I had a feeling that Raquel and Franklyn were somehow intertwined in this mystery. They were both part of the same stage play, and even if they weren't close, they surely spent some time together, and maybe finding him would help me find out what happened to Raquel. I decided to take the case.

"Payment's not necessary," I said. "I can try and help

117

you out, at least for a little bit. Do you think Maria would mind if I looked through her apartment?"

"I don't think looking through her apartment would do you any good, to be honest. I think you'd be better off looking through his apartment."

"Oh, my mistake. I had assumed the two of them were living together."

"Nope, they don't. They still live separately."

"No problem whatsoever. I'm certainly not judging them for it. Will we have to talk to the landlord to get access to his apartment?"

"Nope, I have a copy of his apartment key."

"Where does he live?"

"In Fife. Give me your number so I can text you the address."

We exchanged numbers and she then texted me the address. After confirming I received it, I said to her, "Okay. I guess I'll meet you up there. Is Maria going to come along?"

"I think it's best if we let her rest at her place for now. She's been through a lot lately. If we find anything, I'll be back to tell her."

"Fair enough," I said. "Let's get going."

CHAPTER 5

After performing the usual ritual of placing my phone in the charger and placing my briefcase in the backseat, I rode with my ghostly companion over to Fife, trying to follow Elizabeth as well as possible, but not fretting about it since I had the address punched into the phone and the navigator would guide me should we get separated.

"Vinnie?" Raquel said, breaking the silence of the car trip. "Why are we visiting Elizabeth's brother's apartment?"

"I have a feeling we're going to find something there. I think we'll find something that could help us with your case."

"Oh. I suppose that's a bit of a relief. I thought for a moment that you had forgotten that you're supposed to find out why I died and not why her brother is missing."

"I'd never forget about you, Raquel." We shared a glance and both smiled.

"That's kind of you to say, Vinnie, I'm flattered. Still

119

though, what do you expect to find there?"

"I'm not sure. I'm hoping there's a link between you and Franklyn. The two of you were in *A Pirate, An Officer, and a Princess* together, and both of you went missing at the same time. There's a good chance that the two cases are somehow linked."

"I suppose that makes sense."

"If nothing else, it's something to look into right now. If this turns out to be a bust, I'm probably going to go back to Ed and see if he's heard anything from Officer Martinez. Ed might think I'm crazy, but he's still a good man and a good friend. I'm sure he'd help me out if I asked. Otherwise, I'll check to see when the Lakewood Playhouse is open and see if I can talk to some of the staff or the actors there to see if we can find more information. So I do have other ideas, I just wanted to cross this one out before moving on."

"Are you sure it's not because you've fallen for Elizabeth?"

"Raquel, you know you're the only one for me."

She glared at me for a few moments as I gave her a wide-eyed, large, open mouthed goofy grin. Eventually, her defense cracked and she began laughing uproariously. I joined in the cacophony and we both exchanged a little bit of small talk as we drove on to Franklyn's apartment complex.

We arrived at the Granite Apartment complex, a four-story gray building with a drab exterior and an even duller interior. I never knew that a place could be so gray or that there were that many shades of gray, but as soon as I entered and noticed the slight variations of hues between the walls and the floors, I was convinced I had never seen such an uninspired color scheme.

Franklyn's room was on the first floor. Raquel decided to take this opportunity to float directly from this floor to the floor above us, and as Elizabeth and I were walking down the hallway, my ghostly companion could not resist suddenly appearing upside down in front of me from the floor above screaming "Boo!" as I passed by.

I jumped a bit, and when Elizabeth stared at me, confused, I simply said, "Sorry, I thought I heard something." She continued to stare for a moment, and opened her mouth for a second and held her hand up near her head, index finger extended, as if she had something to say. She seemed to think better of it, turned around, and continued towards her brother's room. I followed her until we reached room number fifteen.

"I have to admit," I said to Elizabeth as she began to unlock her brother's door. "I find it a bit quaint that Maria and Franklyn are living separately, especially after they have been dating for what, two or three years? Don't get me wrong, I'm not criticizing. I actually like it. It's very traditional."

"Well, I'm not sure that it's because either of them are traditional," Elizabeth explained. "But I think it has more to do with Franklyn's commitment issues. I actually talked to him about it last weekend. I seemed to have gotten through to him. Who knows? Maybe the two of them will be living together very soon."

I smiled at her as she opened the door. To say either of us were not prepared for what we saw would be like saying the inland taipan was a mildly poisonous snake. The two of us stood there dumbfounded, trying desperately to process what we had just seen.

CHAPTER 6

When I opened the door, I was awestruck by the scene before us. It was something I could have never anticipated. Photographs. Photographs everywhere. On mantels, on tables, on walls and on floors. Some in heart shaped frames, some in the traditional square, some in an oval. All of them of either Raquel by herself or Raquel and a man—with reddish brown hair and an athletic build, wearing what appeared to be an old officer's uniform—on a stage together. It was easy to infer that it was Franklyn with Raquel. A montage of photographs of Raquel was on a display board tacked onto the light blue apartment wall on the east side, a virtual shrine to the now deceased actress.

"Oh…my…God…." Elizabeth was dumbfounded.

"Yeah. I know." That was all I could muster.

"Imagine that," Raquel said. "I guess he must really admire me."

"This…doesn't look good, does it?" asked Elizabeth.

123

"No, I can't say it does," I said in return.

"There must be a reasonable explanation for this though, right? I mean, it can't be what it looks like."

"Y—yeah, of course. I'm sure there must be a reasonable explanation."

"Maybe…maybe he was organizing some pictures of Raquel, and left in the middle of it because he had to leave for his trip. Maybe?"

"His trip that had been cancelled…."

"Okay, I know that doesn't make any sense. It just—it can't be what it looks like!"

"Hmm. What does it look like to you, Vinnie?" asked Raquel. "He just admires me, that's all."

"There's a not so thin line between admiration and obsession, though," I said.

"I know," Elizabeth said sternly. "And I admit on the surface it looks like he has crossed the line."

"I think the two of you are overreacting," Raquel said. "It's actually kind of sweet, when you think about it. He loves me so much he always wants to see me, that's all."

"It's one thing to love someone, it's another to be a maniac about it," I said to Raquel.

"Okay, I get it," Elizabeth said, clearly upset. "You don't need to rub it in. I get it, it's really creepy."

"I'm sorry, I didn't mean to—"

"It's okay, Vincent. I understand. It's just, he's still my brother. I just refuse to believe it is what it seems until I get a chance to speak with him, or at the very least we find more definitive proof. At the very least, I just—I just want to at least fool myself into thinking he's not some creepy stalker."

"All right," I said. "That makes sense. I think we should look around a bit more and see if we can find anything. We still don't know where he's at, and why he's not responding to your texts. Maybe we can find some clues here."

"Yeah, all right. Good plan."

We began a thorough search of the room. As we searched, I could occasionally hear Elizabeth muttering to herself, chastising her brother as she looked. "Jesus, Franklyn. These are just photos of the two of you in a play. Why are you putting that in a heart shaped frame?"

It was odd. All of the pictures were either of Raquel by herself or moments in the play, various scenes where their two characters were on stage together. One of the odd things about the pictures, though, was that the way Raquel was posed in them kind of suggested that they were selfies. It didn't quite add up. Why did Franklyn have Raquel's selfies? It didn't make sense. Unless, of course, he had somehow stolen her phone and stolen her pictures.

As I walked towards his bedroom I noticed something beneath my feet. I looked down towards the parquet floor and saw that I was stepping on red flower petals. These petals led from just outside the bedroom to Franklyn's bed. When I walked into the room, the first thing that struck me was that hanging just over his bed was a large, framed picture of Raquel. After a few stunned seconds of staring, I allowed my eyes to move down to the bed, where I saw more red flower petals spread all over his covers.

Elizabeth followed me not too long after, and almost immediately upon entering the room, she did an about face and left. "Nope, sorry. I can't do this right now. Vincent, please keep looking for me and find something that can help us find my brother. I've got to get out of here." I looked behind me and saw Elizabeth hurrying out the bedroom door and into the living room, slamming the door behind her.

"Poor girl," I said to myself. I looked forward again and saw Raquel floating in front of the large picture. Her reaction was a bit odd, though. At first I thought she was upset, which would have been the more natural reaction. Instead, she seemed, for lack of a better term, flattered.

"Wow, the man really seems to admire me, doesn't he, Vincent?" Raquel asked.

"I don't think it's admiration, Raquel," I said. "I think you are misunderstanding what's going on here."

"And I think the two of you are being silly," Raquel said. "Gestures like this are a very considerate way of showing people you care. People just tend to overreact over actions they don't understand, that's all."

"You're taking this a little too well, Raquel," I said.

"It's okay to be upset."

"Why would I be upset, though?"

"I think you just don't understand what's going on, Raquel. I think you're misunderstanding—"

"I don't think I'm misunderstanding anything. I know what the two of you are thinking, and I simply disagree. This isn't nearly as bad as the two of you are making it out to be."

I paused. I didn't know what to say. I knew, at the very least, that trying to convince her otherwise at this point was futile. Instead of arguing, I said meekly, "Okay, Raquel, if you say so."

"I do. Everything is all right."

With a heavy sigh, I decided that the only course of action I could take was to explore the rest of the apartment and see if there were any clues there that could help me locate Franklyn's whereabouts.

I continued to look around the room. My attention turned towards the window that was along the wall on the same side as the headboard of the bed. It was slightly ajar, and I noticed scratch marks on the window sill and underneath the window. I tried to shut the window completely, but it refused to close.

Mentally shrugging it off, I continued to explore the rest of the room, but was unable to find anything out of the ordinary—other than the large photograph and flower petals, of course. But ignoring that, as difficult as it was, everything else looked like a typical young man's bedroom. Having come up empty in my search, I decided to leave. As I did so, I approached Elizabeth, who was waiting for me in the living room with her arms crossed, pacing slightly.

"Did you find anything else?" Elizabeth asked hesitatingly.

"Nothing that could lead us to Franklyn, unfortunately," I said. "I did notice his bedroom window was busted open. Do you know what that's all about?"

"Oh shit, that window," Elizabeth said, uncrossing her arms and snickering a bit to herself. "Yeah, Franklyn told me all about it. So not this last Saturday, but the Saturday before that, the cast of that play he's in had a late night production, so they decided to get some drinks after the play was over. They had apparently found this low key dive bar that was pretty lax when it came to checking ID or whatever. I don't know, I'm just basing this of what my brother was telling me. Anyway, my brother gets so plastered that he can't even drive himself home. He gets a ride from one of the other cast members, but when he gets home, he realizes that he forgot his keys in the playhouse's locker. Apparently they have some lockers there so cast members can put their things in there while they are on stage.

"Now, perhaps he should have called me up, but that wouldn't have helped. I didn't have a key to his apartment at the time. Maybe he should have called Maria. I'm not sure if she has a key to his apartment either, but even if she did, he had a reason for not calling her. She was fast asleep, as she had to work early the next morning, and Franklyn had promised her he wouldn't drink anymore until his twenty-first birthday, as — well, let's just say my brother tends to drink to excess.

"I don't know what you would do in this situation, but let me tell you what my idiot brother did. He decided the best course of action would be to break into his own room. He got in all right, but you can see at what cost. Apparently it wasn't even him that actually broke in, but the friend who drove him home. He wouldn't tell me who, though. He wanted to protect his identity, apparently. His friend learned how to break in from a book or something he read online. Kind of scary if you think about it.

"Franklyn called me up the next morning to get me to drive him to the playhouse, and to keep this thing a secret from Maria. It's actually why I have a spare key now. We got it from a locksmith that same morning, as I wanted to make sure this didn't happen again. He actually swore me to secrecy, and apparently had his friend do the same thing. But considering the circumstances, I think it's appropriate for me to tell you this information."

"I'm sure he wouldn't mind, all things considered," I confirmed. "He should probably get that window fixed, though. He's pretty vulnerable to home invasions at this point."

"I've told him the same thing, but he says he can't

129

afford it right now."

"His landlord won't pay for the damages?"

"I mean, it is his fault, and his landlord, Francesca, she's a really good friend of ours. He doesn't want to take advantage of her good nature. Besides, if he ever tried to pull the wool over her eyes I'd kick his sorry ass—and he knows it too." Elizabeth then flexed her noodle arm in a mock show of strength. "If you met Francesca, you'd understand."

"I'll have to meet her then. Anyway...," I said, rubbing the back of my neck. "Unfortunately, other than the obvious, there doesn't really seem to be anything too unusual about his apartment. At least, I couldn't find anything that could lead me to where he is currently."

"Yeah, I couldn't find anything either. So, where do we go from here?"

"I'm not quite sure," I confessed. "But I'm sure I'll think of something. I can always make a few calls or talk to a buddy I know on the police force. Maybe I could give the playhouse or his workplace a call in the morning and find out more."

"Okay, sounds good. I'd have to look up that information at home, but I think I can dig it up for you."

"Thank you. With that, I think we're done here. Let's get going."

My hand was about to be placed on the door when Elizabeth suddenly grabbed my hand—a not too unpleasant feeling, I might add.

"Hey, Vincent, wait a second. Let me do something really quickly." She immediately turned around, pulled down the montage, and began gathering all of the picture frames around the house.

"Elizabeth, what the hell are you doing?" I asked rather sternly.

"Look, it's not like I'm trying to hide evidence or anything. I just...." She paused, frames in hand. "I just.... Until we know exactly what's going on, I don't want people to find — well, all of this." She held the frames in one hand and gestured with the other, which caused her to fumble the frames a bit in her hand. But luckily, she was able to recover and get her second hand under them just before she dropped everything. "Excuse me. I mean, in case this isn't what it looks like, you know? I'm just going to put all of these pictures in a drawer, and maybe hide the big one in the closet. Oh, and I want to clean up the rose petals too."

"Elizabeth, we really shouldn't be messing with this place."

"It's not actually a crime scene, though, is it, Vincent?" she asked, having put the frames in her arms in an empty kitchen drawer. "Besides, if it turns out — you know — that Franklyn is guilty of the worst, I'd back you up on everything. I'll even let the cops know it was my idea to put everything away. Hell, I'll tell them I did it behind your back. Maybe I'll just tell them I overpowered you, I don't know. I just...." She paused, looking down and arms extended, placing her hands on the edge of the kitchen table. "I just can't bear the idea of my parents wondering what's going on and deciding to visit Franklyn, only to see—well, what we saw. I don't need my parents seeing all of that. He's the baby of the family, you know?"

"Ah, what the hell?" I said while shrugging my shoulders, "What do I care? I'm not a cop, and like you said, it's not a crime scene. I suppose technically no crime has actually been committed. Even if your brother is guilty of—well, you know—technically, it's not illegal to have a bunch of pictures lying around the house." As creepy as that might be, I thought to myself.

"Awesome! I'm glad you see it my way. Thanks, Vincent. Now, help me put these pictures away."

We searched the rest of the house and gathered every photograph of Raquel, or Franklyn and Raquel, and tried to place them in whatever unused drawers we could find. Luckily, one of Franklyn's dresser drawers was empty, so we were able to place the majority of the pictures there.

That drawer couldn't fit all of them, though, so we wound up placing a couple of them in the closet with the oversized picture that had been hanging on the wall. It took a meticulous team effort to take down the large photograph hanging over Franklyn's bed, especially on my part, because all her bravado aside, joking, false, or otherwise, Elizabeth was not a physically strong woman, so I had to take on most of the load.

Picking up the rose petals seemed to take ages. We

couldn't find a vacuum cleaner or a Dustbuster, and weren't even sure if either of those tools would have really helped us out much. Instead, we had to gather them by hand, and make constant trips to the garbage can to dispose of them.

During all of this, I had to ignore Raquel's protests. For some reason, she found it odd that we were putting away all of these pictures, and insisted that Elizabeth and I were overreacting over nothing. Obviously, because of where I was and what we were doing, I couldn't exactly hold a conversation with her. I did let out a few barely audible and scolding remarks such as, "We'll talk later!" and "Not now! I'll talk to you after we're done!" This did draw a few bewildered glances from Elizabeth, but she ultimately ignored me and continued with her work.

"Thank you very much for all of your help," Elizabeth said as she reached for the apartment door, the two of us having finished a relatively clean sweep of the apartment—which was, I must say, quite a painstaking effort. "And thanks for your understanding. This is kind of difficult for me, you know? I really didn't expect all of this when I got up this morning. A brother who turns out to be missing, and his apartment looking like something out of *Silence of the Lambs*. I'm just a little confused right now, that's all."

"I understand. I'm glad I could help." Elizabeth flashed a sincere smile for the first time since I met her. "Anyway," I continued, "We should get going. We still have time; we still might be able to find your brother, or at least find out where he's at."

With a silent nod, Elizabeth opened the door and we exited the apartment.

While Elizabeth had her back to me as she locked the apartment door, a dumpy, middle aged woman with brown hair mixed with gray, wearing a black and white striped sweater with tight pants, was waddling from the stairwell over towards us. Not thinking much of it, I simply nodded and muttered, "How's it going?" But I noticed rather quickly the woman wasn't looking at me as much as she was looking past me, her eyes focused on my lovely companion.

"Elizabeth?" the chubby woman asked. "Is that you?"

Elizabeth turned around quickly. "Francesca!" she hollered, a noise she followed up with a high-pitched squeal. The two women embraced as Elizabeth continued by screaming, "Oh my God! It is so good to see you!"

"You as well. You're looking really good, Elizabeth. I was just passing by, and when I heard the door open, I thought Franklyn had returned, so I wanted to say hello to him. Imagine my surprise when I saw you instead."

"Wait a second," I said to Francesca. "You know where Franklyn ran off to?"

"Um, yes, I do. I don't believe I've had the pleasure, young man. What's your name?" She extended her hand out towards me.

"Sorry about that. I'm Vincent Pietro. Elizabeth and I

are looking for Franklyn."

"Francesca Tyler. It is a pleasure to meet you, Vincent. It's so good that Elizabeth has finally found a handsome young man like you."

"Oh. Uh—we're not dating, Francesca," Elizabeth explained. "He's a private investigator."

"Oh really? Well, that's too bad. She is single, though, Vincent, in case you are interested."

Elizabeth sighed, smiled meekly at me, and shrugged, and after a second's pause, I said, "I'll keep that in mind, ma'am."

"So, you said you are a private investigator, Vincent. What brings you over here? Has Franklyn gone missing?"

"It appears to be that way," I explained.

"He's working on a missing persons case for the police, and searching for a girl named Raquel Cobb," Elizabeth continued to explain. "She's actually a good friend of Maria's. However, right now we're looking for Franklyn. Do you know where he's at?"

"Yes, he told me he was going to a cabin with Maria. He said he planned on having a romantic weekend with her. It sounded like a lot of fun to me."

"Oh shit," Elizabeth said. "So he went to the cabin after all."

"The one in Evergreen?" I asked Elizabeth.

"Yeah. He must have gone there even though the trip was cancelled."

"So he told you he was headed over there?" I asked

Francesca.

"Yes. I ran into him just before he left. He asked me to keep an eye on his apartment, and I said of course, I knew all about his hunting trip, and it'd be no problem for me to keep an eye out for him. He then told me no, his hunting trip had been cancelled, so he and Maria were going to use the cabin for themselves. Their anniversary is coming up soon, and apparently Maria had told him she wanted to meet him at the cabin as an early romantic getaway, and a celebration of sorts. I encouraged the two of them to do so. Young people should have fun together while they have time." Francesca paused and looked at us, perplexed. I felt my blood run cold. "Are you guys okay? Elizabeth, you look pale as a ghost."

"Francesca," Elizabeth explained. "Maria is at her apartment right now. Until I visited her this morning, she thought that Franklyn was up at the cabin hunting with our uncle. Hell, until I called my uncle up this morning, I thought the same thing. Maria did not ask Franklyn to go to the cabin."

"Are you sure?" Francesca asked. "What am I asking? Of course you are. But it just doesn't make any sense. He said it was Maria's idea. Why would he say this?"

"Perhaps because he wanted to hide what he was really doing," I thought aloud, creating an awkward silence among the three of us.

"Oh my God," Elizabeth said. "The mysterious man Raquel was excited about. You don't think it was

Franklyn, do you? Maybe she didn't realize that he was—you know—and maybe when he said Maria, he was actually talking about—"

"I don't know," I said, cutting off Elizabeth. "All I know is something strange is going on." Turning towards Elizabeth, I asked, "Do you have an extra key to the cabin?"

"Yes, of course I do," she said in response. "Everyone in the family has a key. Is that where we're headed next?"

"It's where I am heading next," I explained. "You are staying here."

"Bullshit—I'm going with you. He's my brother, I want to find him too."

"I understand, but you need to tell Maria about Franklyn, and you need to stay with her so she doesn't do anything crazy."

"Like hell I am. I'm not telling her what we found in there."

"That's not what I meant. I just want you to assure her that we're looking for him. Also, there's still a chance that Franklyn will return home, either back to his place or Maria's. I need you to let me know if he returns."

"I suppose that makes sense," Elizabeth said.

"Also, I'm worried this trip could be dangerous. You saw his room. I'm not sure what sort of mindset he's in right now."

"His room?" Francesca asked. "Is there something wrong with his room?"

"I'll…I'll talk to you about it later, Francesca," Elizabeth said. "Vincent, you're not planning on hurting my brother, are you?"

"No. Absolutely not. I'm not going to play hero. If I see him and it seems dangerous, I'll call the police and get out of there. You're going to have to trust me on this one."

"I don't know."

"What's going on?" asked Francesca. "Did Franklyn do something wrong?"

"Not now, Francesca!" Elizabeth screamed, followed immediately by, "Oh shit, I'm sorry, Francesca. I didn't mean it. It's just…. Honestly, I'll talk to you later, Francesca. Trust me, okay?"

"Okay…okay, if you say so."

"Look, Elizabeth," I continued, my hands placed on her shoulders, "I don't want you to come along because I've done enough of these cases to learn that family just complicates things. I've done this before. I'm a neutral party to this. I can be trusted to react appropriately. I just don't want you to get hurt. I couldn't live with myself if something happened to you."

Elizabeth stared at me for a moment in a stunned silence. Slowly, an emotion overtook her being, and her facial expression clearly changed. It went from a subdued melancholy to overwhelming blitheness as the woman began to laugh hysterically in my face. My hands moved sheepishly off her shoulders back down to my sides.

"I'm sorry, I don't mean to laugh, but how long have you known me, man? That's a little melodramatic, wouldn't you say?"

"I guess. It seemed like the right thing to say at the time. I just meant I don't want you to get hurt."

"I mean, don't get me wrong, I appreciate the sentiment, and you're right, it sounds dangerous, and it's my brother. I'm not sure what I could even do if it turns out that he is a psychopath. I don't want to deal with that, so I have no problem staying here. It's just the way you said it. You couldn't live with yourself. Come on, dude. You've known me for a few hours at most."

"I'm sorry. I didn't mean anything by it. I just said the first thing that popped into my head."

"I know, I know, I'm sorry too. It just surprised me, that's all. Anyway, let me take the key off the ring." She took a large key off her key ring and handed it to me. She then said, "I have the address saved somewhere on my phone. Let me look for a second. Yes, here it is, I'll text it to you now."

After hearing a beep on my phone, I looked down and acknowledged that I received the text.

"You'll turn into a secluded road that'll eventually just end. Somewhere around there you should be able to see a sign for the Sercombe Trail. Just follow it, and eventually you'll reach the cabin. My brother actually knows of a road through the woods that can get you to the cabin directly, but I'm afraid I'm not familiar with it.

139

I'm not over there nearly as often as Franklyn."

"That's okay, as long as I can get there. You said the Sercombe Trail, right? I think I can remember that. Okay, I think it's time for me to go. Thanks for your help, Elizabeth."

When I was about to head off on my journey, I gave Elizabeth an awkward "not quite sure if we should hug but a handshake seems like a kind of weird sort of thing" before I simply settled on waving goodbye. As I headed down the steps, I could overhear Francesca say, "I think the two of you would make an awfully nice couple."

Walking down the steps, a certain voice began to penetrate my consciousness. For a short period of time I had managed to successfully tune out my ghostly companion, as she mostly was voicing various complaints and expressing ire towards me for ignoring her in favor of Elizabeth. Even if I had wanted to respond to everything she said, there really hadn't been a good time. Entering the car with her floating in right next to me finally afforded me the opportunity to address all the objections she had.

"...and right now, I can say pretty much whatever I want to you because you are just going to ignore me. Yes, just ignore the poor spirit who is desperately looking for help. Just ignore me. I bet you won't even notice if I remind you that I did see you naked and know that you have a microscopic —"

"I can hear you, you know," I said, interrupting

her rant. After placing it back into the charger, I began plugging the address of the cabin into my phone.

"Well, look who's finally acknowledging me," Raquel said without breaking her stride. "It's nice to know that I hadn't turned invisible to you."

As I backed up the car and began my journey to Evergreen, I said, "What did you want me to do? I was talking to Elizabeth, and there really wasn't a good opportunity to pull out my Bluetooth and pretend that I was on the phone. If I started talking to you in the middle of our conversation, I would have looked schizophrenic."

"I didn't like the way she was looking at you. And…." Her voice became gruffer as she said the next part. "I didn't like the way you were looking at her."

"What? What do you mean? How were we looking at each other?"

"You know, all lovey dovey and googly-eyed."

"Even if we were, what do you care?"

"She's just not good for you, that's all. A handsome man like you deserves much better than a weird, ugly looking slut like her."

"Ouch, Raquel, that's pretty harsh. I didn't even think you knew words like that."

"She even laughed at you when you said you couldn't live with yourself if she got hurt. Imagine that, a woman who doesn't appreciate a gentleman. What kind of woman laughs at a man who pours his heart out like that?"

141

"She had a point. I was being a little melodramatic."

"I found it very sweet. She doesn't deserve a man like you."

"I appreciate the sentiment, but it's not like we're dating or anything. I only just met her, and I'm only interested in finding her brother, Franklyn."

"Why are we looking for Franklyn, anyway? Have you forgotten that you're supposed to be trying to find out why I died, and not why Franklyn is missing?"

"Not at all. Why do you think I want to find Franklyn in the first place?"

"You're doing it for your girlfriend Elizabeth, whom you love so much."

"Stop it. What's gotten into you?" I then muttered to myself, "You're acting like a petulant child."

"What did you say?" Raquel screamed.

"Nothing, nothing at all," I said, still grumbling to myself.

"I'm sorry, but being dead is a little bit stressful, you know? So I apologize if I'm not the model of maturity every waking moment of the day! And forgive me for asking whether you've forgotten what you were doing when it seems like we've gotten off the beaten track!"

"Look!" I screamed. "You saw all the creepy photographs in Franklyn's apartment. You saw how weird that was! I'm trying to find Franklyn because I'm sure if we find him, we'll find you!" My voice began to crack a little as I repeated myself, much more softly, "I'm sure if we find him, we'll find you."

"What do you mean by that?" Raquel asked.

"You know what I mean. Don't make me say it."

"Oh, so you mean you think Franklyn…. Oh…."

"Yeah." With that, I placed my key in the ignition and started the car. We began what felt like the longest journey of my life.

CHAPTER 7

We sat there in silence for a long while. The only sounds that could be heard were the other vehicles on the road passing us by, my car's engine, and the occasional chime of my GPS. I didn't know what to say. I had no idea whether I'd upset the girl, or whether the gravity of the situation had finally penetrated her psyche. I tried several times to say something, to think of something comforting to say, but every time I opened my mouth no words could be formed.

"So you never actually forgot about me," Raquel said, piercing the awkward silence.

"What do you mean?"

"I thought you forgot about me. I thought that you were more concerned with Elizabeth, and that was why you were looking for her brother Franklyn."

"I'd be lying if I said I didn't want to find him as well, but that doesn't mean I forgot about you, Raquel. In fact, part of the reason I agreed to search Franklyn's

144

apartment in the first place was because I think there is a link between the two of you, and that by finding him we could find out what happened to you too. Both of you were part of the same play, and both of you went missing at the same time. It seems like more than a coincidence."

"I apologize then, Vinnie. I really thought you had forgotten all about me. That's why I got upset at you. I'm sorry for that."

"Uh, that's quite all right, Raquel. It's just I thought you'd be more upset over what I found in his apartment. You know, Franklyn's obsession with you."

"Oh that. Sorry, Vinnie. I simply think you and Elizabeth are wrong. Franklyn did not murder me, and he did not have an unhealthy obsession with me. In fact, seeing his apartment jogged some memories that I had forgotten."

"But Raquel, what about the photographs spread all over the apartment? What about the rose petals? The virtual shrine he had over his bed?"

"Vinnie, we all have different ways of expressing love. Just because the way he expressed his love is unconventional and might be deemed bizarre by society at large does not mean that there was anything wrong with what he did. I think it was simply Franklyn's way of showing his adoration for me."

"I think it went a little bit further than mere adoration."

"Think about it, Vinnie. I remember that Franklyn loved me, but he couldn't tell anybody. He was simply

145

too nice to break up with his girlfriend Maria, but he wanted to see me, desperately. So he came up with a way to allow himself to do that, if only at home. Unusual? Perhaps, but nothing inherently malevolent about it, wouldn't you say?"

Denial is not just a river in Egypt, I thought to myself. Instead, I bit my tongue and said, "I'm afraid I'm going to have to highly disagree with you on that one, Raquel."

"Now that I think about it, I think going to the cabin is a complete waste of time. The cabin's probably empty. We're certainly not going to find me or Franklyn there, that's for sure."

"No, too much of it ties together for it to be simply a coincidence. Elizabeth saw it too. Both of you disappeared at the same time. You told your parents about a new man in your life, but were very vague about it. Franklyn's photographs of you are spread throughout his apartment. No, too much seems to connect."

"You'll see. I'm sure Franklyn didn't murder me."

"No offense, Raquel, but how can you be sure? What do you remember about him?"

"The Franklyn I knew was completely different than the one Elizabeth described and the one you think he was. He was one of the nicest men I ever met. He was so kind. So sweet. So understanding and dutiful. He could be a little over the top at times, I remember, and had a bit of a temper, but I knew he always meant well. He was so very smart as well. He impressed me with his vast intellect.

146

Franklyn was so in love with me, too, it was so obvious. The only reason he never acted on it was because he was dating Maria, and I always felt that he stayed with her out of a sense of duty. Still, every time we met he told me he loved me, and wanted to be with me forever. It was actually very romantic, now that I think about it."

"I don't know, Raquel. I understand what you are saying, but what we've found so far is just so unsettling and disturbing. The evidence points to Franklyn doing something very wrong. At the very least, you have to admit that it's worrying. It's incredibly worrying."

"I think you are overreacting, Vinnie. Are you sure we need to see the cabin?"

"Yes, I'm sure. Maybe you're right. Maybe there is nothing there. I'll give you permission to laugh at me if I'm wrong, but we've got to know. We've got to check."

"Okay, Vinnie," she said with a sigh. "We can visit the cabin if you think it'll be worthwhile. I suppose since we're already on our way we might as well keep going."

We remained silent the rest of the trip except for a few words here or there. For the most part, though, I didn't say anything. What could I say? So much had happened during such a short time, and with Raquel simply refusing to believe what seemed exceedingly obvious to me, I again found myself in a position where I was struggling to think of anything appropriate to say. Thus, once again, for the majority of the trip, the only sounds accompanying us were the sounds of the road and my navigator, while the sun faded out of view as day turned into night.

The small town of Evergreen was beautiful at night. The town really seemed to glow for some reason. True, the town was for the most part like any other suburban town. It had convenience stores, fast food places, restaurants and hotels like you would find in any other suburban setting. Perhaps a little more peaceful and a little less populated than average, but otherwise relatively unremarkable. Yet, somehow, that night I could not help but notice how brightly the lights seemed to shine, and just how serene the scene seemed to be, a stark contrast to what I was feeling internally.

Except for a quick respite for a meal and the alleviation of my bodily fluids, we drove right past that town. The main thoroughfare of Evergreen wasn't the destination — our destination was the forest area right on the outskirts of town. We continued our silent excursion to the forest and drove past the winding empty roads. For large stretches the only illumination was my headlights.

My GPS had us turn onto a secluded road that cut into the forest, a road that I nearly passed. But luckily I was able to stop just in time, and it must have been quite a sudden stop because for a moment my ghostly companion was ahead of me just outside the car. She returned back to the passenger seat, giggling all the way. Even I appreciated the comedy of the moment.

As we headed into the forest, I felt the ominous

loom of the trees hovering over us. It felt cold, unfeeling, and oppressive, as if the trees themselves were telling us to turn around. Only slightly daunted, I continued cautiously down the road until I reached the end.

"I don't see a cabin around here, Vinnie," Raquel said, exiting the car and floating around.

"According to Elizabeth," I said, "There should be a sign for the Sercombe Trail somewhere around here. Sercombe Trail. Okay, I'll take a look." I took my phone out of its car charger. I also went into the back seat and picked up my briefcase, mostly out of habit. After shaking the phone to take advantage of its flashlight, I began examining the woods looking for the sign.

Instead of the sign, though, I saw something that I had not noticed when I initially reached the end of the road. A red Honda Civic was parked completely on the opposite side of the road from where I had parked, on the edge of the forest almost in a ditch. I must have missed it because I was driving on the left side of the road, disobeying all rules of the road. However, I had figured, mostly correctly, that it did not matter where I drove because nobody else would be using this road.

Wordlessly, I walked over to the vehicle and began a cursory examination. I placed my hand on the hood. It was ice cold. It must have been there for a while. I was contemplating what this could mean when I suddenly heard Raquel call out to me.

"Vinnie! I've found it! The trail is over here!"

149

I turned around and saw the sign that was behind my car and to its left, the exact opposite direction from where I had been looking. Admittedly, Raquel finding the trail made me lose my train of thought, so as soon as she called, I was no longer thinking about the Civic.

"Thanks, Raquel! Good eyes! Now, let's see where this trail takes us."

As I walked down the forest trail, a gradual nervousness began to creep over me. Here I was, alone save for a ghostly companion that nobody could see or hear but me. Slowly it dawned on me that if I ran into a psychopath or a murderer or some other weirdo on the trail, I'd have no way to defend myself. The various animal noises I heard in the forest abyss did not help my confidence at all, and with the trees looming over me with branches that appeared to be little hands covering the night sky, it made for a truly unnerving scene. At that moment I wished I really had that revolver that I had threatened to shoot myself with that morning, rather than having just made it up.

"This forest is kind of scary, wouldn't you agree, Vinnie?" Raquel asked, cutting through the silence like a hot butter knife. "I wouldn't blame you if you just wanted to turn around and go home." I turned to my right to see her bright, shining, smiling face. "I'm just kidding, of course."

"Of course," I said.

"Don't worry, Vinnie, no need to be scared. If

anything comes at you, I'll protect you. Well, I suppose I can't really do that, but I promise to scream very loudly."

"I'm not scared, Raquel," I protested.

She paused for a second and observed my gradual gait through the forest. "I can clearly tell you're not afraid." Raquel was giggling as she said this.

I have to admit, having Raquel floating over my right shoulder and talking to me did make me feel a little bit better. Not that she could have protected me if something had attacked me, mind you, as she even admitted. But still, having a companion there to talk to me made me feel less alone and more in control of my environment. Granted, this didn't really quicken my pace any.

We continued to share a bit of small talk as I made my way through the trail. For a small moment, I began to have reservations that I was not headed in the correct direction. True, Elizabeth had told me to just follow the trail, but it seemed like I had been walking for a while, and I wondered whether she had forgotten a part where she might have gone off the trail to find the cabin. I also began to get nervous about whether I could actually find my way back to the car. At the very least, I began to question how intelligent it was for me to engage in this expedition at night, and whether I should have brought Elizabeth after all.

All of my apprehensions turned into relief when I saw the cabin at the end of my deliberate and hesitant journey through the forest trail.

"Ah, finally," I said. "We're finally here, Raquel."

As I walked towards the cabin my periphery vision caught a glimpse of a white pickup truck, presumably a Ford, parked just outside the cabin. My mind was on other things, though, so I ignored the vehicle and continued towards the cabin, walking up the steps leading to the door, Raquel close behind as usual.

I placed my briefcase next to the door. I turned off the flashlight on my phone and placed it in my pocket, as I wanted a free hand to unlock the door. As I reached for the door knob, Raquel, floating, as always, above my right shoulder, shouted, "Wait!"

"Yes? What's wrong?" I turned my head towards my floating companion.

"I'm not sure I actually want to go in there."

I paused and let out a healthy exhale. "I think I understand. The gravity of the situation has finally caught up to you, hasn't it? I should have known that everything you said on the car trip was part of a façade, an attempt to not think about what actually happened."

"Um, it's not that. Vinnie, can I ask you something?"

"Of course."

"I have a secret I need to tell you."

"A secret? You've been keeping something from me? Why?"

"Because it's something very difficult for me to talk about. Believe me, Vinnie, I wanted to tell you earlier, I just couldn't find the words."

152

"Okay, I understand. That's all right, Raquel, don't worry about it. Now, please tell me the secret."

"Do you really want to know?"

"Yes, please tell me."

"Vinnie, knowing might change everything. Are you sure you want to know?"

"Yes, just tell me!" I screamed. I immediately calmed down and followed up by saying, "Sorry. Please, tell me."

"Okay." After a long pause, the girl finally said, "My secret is that I kind of never really wanted to find out how I died. You said I'd disappear when we figured it out, right? I actually kind of knew that from the beginning. I just pretended I didn't know because I didn't want to believe it. It's just—I don't want to disappear. Is it wrong that I kind of just want to stay here and hang around here forever?"

"Wait a second—you really don't want to know why you died?"

"Not really."

"Then why did you come to me in the first place? You asked me why—you specifically asked me why you died."

"It's weird. It's like a voice is telling me to find out, only it's not really a voice, it's more like just a feeling. Like someone is controlling me, telling me what I'm supposed to do. It's like someone is forcing me to. Like someone forced me to come to you. But, I don't really

153

want to know."

"Why didn't you say something before?"

"I don't know. I kind of enjoyed hanging out with you. Now that we're at this cabin — I mean, it's like I'm getting this feeling that we shouldn't do this anymore. I mean, I still have this feeling that we must do it or whatever, but at the same time, I really don't want to open that door, you know? I bet all ghosts have this feeling, though. This feeling that they don't want to solve the mystery, because it means they'd disappear, right?"

After a moment of just staring at Raquel, I rubbed the back of my neck and said, "No, actually. Not at all. Every other ghost has wanted me to solve the mystery, no matter how grisly the truth might have been. Casper, Jill, Melanie — hell, even Naomi. Naomi was the victim of a brutal serial killing. I don't want to remember the things done to that poor woman, so if you thought there was any ghost who wouldn't want to know what happened to them, it would have been her."

"Oh God, Vinnie. What does this mean?" She went down on her feet, her eyes pleading towards me, her face in anguish with her hands curling towards her chest, "What happened to me?" Up until that point, I had never seen a ghost cry. Even when she was upset at me earlier, she didn't actually cry. I reached out to try and comfort her, but alas, my hands went through her, my hands and arms freezing as they did so.

"I'm sorry, Raquel," I said as I backed up a little bit,

trying to cover up the fact that I had just tried to hug a ghost and that I was cold. "I truly am."

"Do we still...?" she said, taking deep breaths between every couple of words. "Do we still have to open the door?"

"It's something we must do, Raquel. We owe it to ourselves. We owe it to Elizabeth. We owe it to Maria. We owe it to Robert and Melinda and everyone else affected by this. Besides," I chuckled, trying to lighten the mood of a somber situation. "Didn't you imply that the feeling is mixed?"

She retorted with, "The bad feeling is kind of winning right now."

"We have to find out, Raquel." I let out a deep sigh. "We have to find out."

As I placed my hand on the knob, I felt a presence. I looked down and saw a pair of ghostly hands form around my chest. I glanced further down and saw parts of her wrists and arms underneath my arm pits, and slowly realized that Raquel had tried to hug me as best her ghostly form could manage. Placing my hands metaphorically on top of hers and physically on my chest, ignoring the bitter cold, I whispered, "I am so, so sorry, Raquel." I closed my eyes for a moment and breathed a couple of heavy sighs. After a short, reflective pause, I moved my hands in order to unlock the door and thrust it open.

My head involuntarily moved back as I closed my

eyes. My right hand swiftly covered my nose and mouth as we opened the door. The smell of death is never something you can get used to, and even if it were, I doubt it would ever be a pleasant smell. I grabbed my briefcase, braved the foul odor, and entered the room. For the first time I envied Raquel, if only for her lack of olfactory receptors.

Other than the pale moonlight that provided woefully little illumination, the room was completely dark. I took out my cell phone once again and shook it in order to activate the flashlight. Raquel left my side and began floating around the room, presumably to examine who or what was in there.

My flashlight moved slowly from the entryway to the center of the room. That is where I saw him, a dead man, lying in the middle of the room. The poor man lay face down on the cabin floor, his left knee curled towards his chest with his left arm tucked underneath his stomach. His right hand was stretched towards me, presumably reaching for the door.

My light moved up and down the man's back, and I noticed a bloody hole that looked like an exit wound from a gunshot. The man was dressed in blue jeans and a letterman jacket. A pool of congealed, cobalt blood lay underneath the body. A blood trail led from the body to the fireplace. I knelt down and gently raised his head to take a better look at his face. There was no mistaking it. The face matched the ones in the photographs of

Franklyn's apartment. The dead man lying underneath my feet was Franklyn Murphy.

"What the hell was wrong with you?" I muttered to myself. I quickly realized I was jumping to conclusions, and decided to continue my examination.

As I moved my flashlight towards the fireplace, I noticed a couple of red high heeled shoes. I paused for a second, closed my eyes, and then continued scanning. I stopped again upon reaching what was clearly a human foot. Sighing deeply, I closed my eyes once again, and then I moved the flashlight towards the rest of the cadaver.

It was a woman's body. I slowly walked up to the body to get a better look. As I stood over the top of her, moving my flashlight to and fro, I was able to get a complete picture. She had brunette hair and silky white skin. Her makeup was faded, but it was clear she had worn ruby red lipstick and coal black mascara around the eyes in an attempt to go for a gothic look. Her white designer dress was covered in blood. Her forehead bore a gash with a rather large wound, and the coagulated blood from that wound had run down her eyes, forming what looked to be tears. "Raquel," I whispered, just loud enough that my companion had doubtlessly overheard what I said.

"Vinnie?" Raquel's voice was heard from somewhere behind me. "Did you call? What is it?"

"Raquel, don't come over here!" I screamed in a futile

157

manner. She was next to me before I could even complete my sentence.

"Oh my God," the poor woman cried. "Oh my God, is that me? Oh God, Vinnie, it's me!"

"I'm so sorry, Raquel. I didn't want you to see this. I didn't want you to see this." I kept repeating that phrase like a mantra as the poor ghost woman went down to her knees and sobbed, with me unable to provide her comfort. I tried holding her, patting her with my hand, anything, but unfortunately nothing I tried worked, for obvious reasons. My flashlight remained fixated on the woman.

"I'm sorry." Raquel began to speak after what seemed like hours. "I'm sorry."

"Don't be," I said, trying to reassure her. "You have nothing to apologize for."

"I don't know what came over me. It's not like I didn't know I was dead. Have you figured out how I died, Vinnie? Or why?"

"Not quite," I said. "I have a theory. You probably know what it is—it has been swimming in my head ever since we searched Franklyn's apartment—but I'm not quite ready to make any definitive conclusions right now. I just want to make sure I've covered everything." I began scanning the room with my flashlight once again.

I looked at the mantle of the fireplace. Something immediately jumped out at me. On top of the mantle were the vestiges of candles melted down to a pile of wax and wicks. These candles surrounded a relatively large, heart shaped picture frame in the middle. I grabbed it with my free hand in order to get a better look. Another photograph of Franklyn and Raquel from when they were in the play. Things continued to appear very incriminating for Mr. Murphy.

My flashlight wandered towards the right of the cabin, one of the few places I hadn't examined yet. I noticed a kitchen table and wandered towards it. The remnants of candles also burnt down to a wick lay on top of the table, as well as some sort of odd, rotted fish meal on two separate plates. Empty wine glasses sat next to each plate, and an unopened bottle of wine sat at the center. An untouched meal intended for two people.

On the floor next to the table were rose petals, the same kind that were in the apartment. I turned around and followed the trail of rose petals until they led me to the opposite side of the cabin to their ultimate destination, a rose covered bed.

I was about to make a declarative statement as to what happened when, after a quick examination of the bed, my flashlight happened upon a nightstand sitting next to it. A desk lamp and a cell phone were the only noticeable items on the stand. I picked up the cell phone with my free hand. It was an Android phone with a pink back cover with a white, flower-like design on the back. Just like the one Maria had described.

The phone was fully charged, as it had been plugged

into the wall. I wondered whether this phone could actually be Maria's. I dismissed the idea at first; she said that she'd lost it, not that it was stolen. Still, it was too much of a coincidence to completely ignore.

I tried to access the phone, but it required me to enter a four-digit passkey which I really should have predicted. At first I didn't know what to do, but then I decided to work under the assumption that it was Maria's phone. If it was her phone though, what could her passkey be? I wondered.

After examining my notes a bit, I remembered something Maria had said to Elizabeth when I interviewed them. She said that her anniversary was a date she could like, never possibly forget. She also said her anniversary was this Saturday. I typed in that date, November 25, aka 1125. Bingo. I was in. There was no doubt in my mind. The phone in my hand was Maria's. What was it doing out here? I wondered.

I skimmed through the phone. A lot of the information was largely uninteresting. There were pictures of Maria and Franklyn, messages to what appeared to be friends and family, and various other applications I couldn't be bothered with exploring further. However, something immediately grabbed my attention. It was the dates and times of the outgoing and incoming phone calls.

There were several incoming and outgoing calls to and from Franklyn, some as recent as only a few days ago, the same time period that Maria said she was missing her phone. There were many texts to Franklyn, but the ones I was interested in were the ones from the period of time the phone was supposedly missing. These series of messages read as follows:

Franklyn: Hey.
Maria: Hi honey!
Franklyn: I have something to ask you.
Maria: What is it?
Franklyn: Ted invited me to a Seahawks-Sounders double header. I told him before I wasn't going to go because of my uncle, but you know, he cancelled. Then Ted invited me out again, and I know I said I'd visit you at the cabin this afternoon, but do you mind if I see you there tonight, after the games?
Maria: Not at all.
Franklyn: Really?
Maria: Really.
Franklyn: Are you sure? You're not mad?
Maria: How could I be mad at you?
Franklyn: You usually find a way, lol, jk. Seriously, though, you are okay with this?
Maria: Of course. In fact, that works out better for me. I'm preparing a surprise for you in Tacoma anyway, and I have some preparations to make at the cabin.
Franklyn: Thanks, babe! You are the best girlfriend ever!
Maria: I don't know. I think Raquel would be a better

girlfriend.

Franklyn: What?

Maria: I mean, to whomever she decided to date, lol.

Franklyn: Oh, that makes sense, lol.

Franklyn: Not true, still, though, you will always be the best girlfriend ever! ☺

Maria: By the way, how do you get to the cabin again?

Franklyn: The address is 4215 Martin Rd SW.

Franklyn: From there you can use some roads through the woods to get to the cabin directly, but that's a bit hard to explain or you can use the GPS and trail, which is much easier to explain.

Maria: Easy way please ☺

Franklyn: GPS will take you to the end of a road.

Franklyn: You're going to have to find the Sercombe Trail.

Maria: That's right. We talked about that earlier over the phone.

Franklyn: Can you get in?

Maria: Don't worry. I can get in.

Franklyn: Elizabeth must have given you the key, then.

Maria: Something like that.

Franklyn: lol I can't believe you forgot my family owned a cabin.

Maria: Sorry. Just been under a lot of stress lately and forgot.

Franklyn: Oh right, your family. Sorry, I hope things

are all right.

Maria: They're fine. Don't worry about it, Raquel's been helping out.

Franklyn: She's a good friend. I should probably get to know her better.

Maria: She's very pretty, isn't she? A great all-around person, wouldn't you say?

Franklyn: lol I guess.

Maria: You know, Raquel doesn't mind hunting, unlike me.

Franklyn: lol, okay. That's cool.

Maria: And she is much smarter, don't you think?

Franklyn: I wouldn't say that. Are you okay? You're acting kind of strange.

Maria: Am I? I don't think I'm acting strange. I'm fine, I think you're reading too much into what I am writing.

Franklyn: lol You are probably right. Anyway, glad you thought of the cabin thing. I'm so excited for tonight.

Maria: Same here. Have fun at the games.

Suddenly, I began to feel cold. At first I thought it was internal, but slowly I realized it was an external chill I felt running down my spine. For a moment I thought that the ghost girl was for some reason touching me, perhaps to get my attention. But soon I noticed what I was really feeling was a slight breeze. I set Maria's phone down and pointed my phone towards the source of the wind. The window was slightly ajar.

I began to walk over to get a better look when I nearly tripped over something. Looking down at my feet, I realized that I had nearly stumbled over a gym bag sitting next to the night stand. Upon further examination of that bag, I noticed that it was full of women's gym clothes stained with dust and other outdoorsy blemishes. Not knowing what to make of this, I scratched my head and continued towards the window.

The window had been tampered with. There were scratch marks on the window sill and underneath the window. I tried to shut the window completely but it refused to do so. I took a glance outside through the window and noticed a steel crowbar lying in the dirt. Something began to reverberate in my head. Elizabeth had told me a friend broke into Franklyn's apartment, not Franklyn himself. She never found out who the friend was, but could it be? I thought to myself. No, it couldn't have been...could it?

I walked over to the body once again. The ghost girl was nowhere to be seen at this point, having presumably floated away looking for clues within the cabin. I bent down on one knee and studied the female corpse a little more closely than I had previously, the initial shock of finding her body having long passed. This time, I noticed her right arm lying next to her side. The reason that this part of her jumped out at me so apparently was that, in her cold, dead fingers, where rigor mortis had already set in, I noticed something—a revolver.

My flashlight moved from her head to a corner of the fireplace. A large patch of blood covered one of the corners of a brick. The corner of the brick matched the pattern of Raquel's bloody wound on her head.

All of the information I had gathered on this case crept into my mind. Maria's phone went missing while Raquel visited her. I found it there in that cabin. There were calls made from that phone during the period of time it had supposedly gone missing. Raquel was an excellent impressionist. She could do a spot-on impression of Maria. Their voices were nearly indistinguishable. Was it possible that Raquel did the calling?

Another thought crept into my mind related to the cell phone. According to the text messages to Franklyn that I had seen, Maria had gotten the key from Elizabeth. No wait — it merely said that she had a way to get in. Then I thought about the broken window. Raquel couldn't possibly have entered that way — but what if she had?

The new man in Raquel's life — I began to think about him. Everyone seemed surprised that she was seeing somebody. I slowly realized that she never actually said the two were dating, or anything quite to that effect. She simply had told her parents that her mystery man was about ready to confess his love.

Wait a second. What exactly did she say? "Every time he saw me he told me he loved me and wanted to be with me forever." My blood ran cold with the realization. I opened the briefcase and pulled out the script to A Pirate,

An Officer, and a Princess. I knelt on one knee as I combed through the play as best I could in the dark. I jumped around the script a bit, and read only bits and pieces of it, but one thing was quite noticeable. Officer Frederick Martin said to Princess Rachelle several times during the course of the play, "I love you…I want to be with you forever."

"I think I know what happened." The apparition's voice came from behind. It startled me a bit, so much I actually dropped the script on the floor. Luckily, I was able to regain composure as I turned around to face the specter. "Imagine that. It looks like you were right," she said, pointing at the dead man. "Franklyn lured me up to the cabin with lewd intentions. He was crazy, obsessed with me even. That's why he had all those photographs of me in his apartment. You know how it was—he kept saying he loved me and that he wanted to be with me forever. I must have rejected him. Of course I did—he was with Maria. And besides, while I did like him a lot, that much is obvious, I didn't truly reciprocate his emotions. When I told him this, he attacked me. He killed me, in fact, but I got him just before he could escape. Yes indeed, that must have been what happened. I can't believe I haven't disappeared yet, though. I solved the mystery, right? Maybe the powers that be want me to stay here. Yep, that must be it. Let's get out of here, Vinnie." She immediately began to float towards the door.

"You and I both know that's not what happened,"

I said somberly. "I can only speculate on the details, but I think I know the gist of what actually occurred here. He didn't lure you out here. Quite the opposite, actually — you lured him out to this cabin. The phone on the nightstand." I pointed over towards the nightstand. "That's your friend's phone. You stole it from her. That's what happened during the celebration. When she supposedly lost her phone, you actually stole it. You probably were able to guess the password the same way I did. She always said that she could never forget her anniversary. It was easy for you to figure it out from there. Dear God, I bet you even knew that she'd be distracted with her family issues. You took advantage of her, Raquel. You took advantage of her friendship and her trust. She took the time out of her day to celebrate your successful audition, even though she was going through some major family turmoil. Yet, you used it as an opportunity to steal her phone." I paused for a moment. I had expected Raquel to say something, perhaps to protest or attempt to justify herself. Instead, I was met with silence.

With a heavy sigh, I continued. "Why you stole her phone in the first place, I'm not sure. Perhaps it was to lure Franklyn to the cabin, but I actually think it was for another reason. In one text message chain in particular, I noticed that in the middle of planning a trip to this cabin Maria suddenly tells Franklyn how awesome Raquel is. It doesn't make much sense why she would do something like that, until you realize that it wasn't Maria saying these things. It was you posing as Maria. I think you stole the phone to drive the two of them apart. However, a different opportunity arose, and you took advantage of that instead. Franklyn was supposed to go on a hunting trip with his uncle. This trip was cancelled when his uncle decided to go to Vegas with his girlfriend. Now, I'm basing this purely off the times on the phone, but I believe Franklin called his girlfriend to let her know that the trip had been cancelled and that he was staying home. She responds that the two of them should go to the cabin to have a romantic getaway together. Unbeknownst to him, though, he never actually called his girlfriend. He was talking to you instead.

"I noticed something when I talked to Maria. You actually do an almost perfect imitation of her voice. To tell the truth, when I first heard her voice, I thought it was you doing your impression again. It is slightly raspier, but the inflexion, the tone, it is perfect. You were a natural actress. Everyone I met praised you for it. Your father remarked that you were an excellent impressionist. You used your talents to fool Franklyn. It was simply a matter of opportunity. You were planning on just breaking the two of them up. However, when he called Maria while you were in possession of her phone, you decided it would be a good time to get Franklyn alone with you in his cabin, away from everyone's prying eyes. To give him a chance to confess the love you were sure he had for you.

"You were the one who broke into his apartment that night when he forgot his keys in the locker of the Lakewood Playhouse. To be honest, I wouldn't be surprised if you actually stole his keys after he took them out of his locker. Maybe he put them down somewhere, or maybe you pickpocketed him, I'm not sure. After getting the keys, you put them back in his locker so you'd have an excuse to break into his apartment. A little farfetched, I admit. I'm probably just being overly cynical at this point. Regardless, it gave you the ability to enter his apartment on the day he was going to meet you in the cabin. You went in through his apartment window, the window you had broken into earlier, in order to decorate his apartment with your photographs. Since Franklyn went to the Seahawks game and the Sounders match, you had plenty of time to do this. I don't know why you did it; my best guess is that you thought this get together was going to go well, and naturally he'd want your picture — or in this case, various pictures. Perhaps it was also a way to 'persuade' him to love you.

"After the games were over, Franklyn went to the cabin expecting his beloved girlfriend. Instead of Maria, though, he saw you here. You broke into the cabin through the window in a similar fashion as to when you broke into Franklyn's apartment. You did this in order to make the following arrangements." My hands gestured around to the whole of the room. I continued. "Now, again, I'm merely speculating here, but I think I know what happened. The candles, the dinner, the rose petals, the bed, the photograph on the mantle — your intentions were quite clear. Elizabeth implied that Franklyn wasn't the brightest bulb. I never knew the man, so I will have to take her word for it. Assuming what she said is true, though, it probably took a moment for Franklyn's poor, weak mind to realize what was happening. He probably spurned your advances. He loved Maria, and would remain loyal to her. He tried to leave." I began to pantomime what I believed happened in this cabin by first walking briskly towards the door. "You jumped in front of him." I turned around at the door. "He told you to move, but you pulled out your gun." I used my right index finger and thumb to mimic a gun. "You walked him over to the fireplace. Maybe you were professing your love, maybe you were threatening him, maybe it was just sheer panic, because everything you had planned for the two of you started to crumble before your very eyes — I don't know. A struggle occurred."

I put my left hand on my right and began mocking a struggle. "In the scuffle, he winds up tossing you to the fireplace — perhaps by accident, perhaps just trying to flee. Before you fall, though, you fire your gun! Bang! I can't tell for certain, but perhaps you didn't even mean to fire. It might have been a reflex. Regardless," I said with a heavy sigh, "You hit your head against the fireplace and were killed. In his last few moments of life,

Franklyn crawled towards the cabin door, but ultimately succumbed to his wounds."

"Huh," the ghost girl said, shrugging a bit with a bemused grin. "Imagine that." Her wounds disappeared, and I could see her unblemished ghost face for the first time as she began to fade.

"Imagine that?" I screamed. "Imagine that. Is that all you have to say?"

"That, and, that was a very entertaining act. You could have been an actor yourself."

"How long?" I asked. "How long did you know you killed Franklyn? Did you know the entire time? Answer me before you go!" I said that last part as if she had a choice.

"I didn't know." She smiled warmly at me. "I kind of remembered while we were on the trip, but I didn't know exactly. Not until I got to this cabin. I kind of pieced everything together when I saw the scene, before you said anything. I didn't know before that, though. Honestly, I didn't. Memory suppression perhaps, I don't know. Maybe part of the 'Swiss' cheese memory. Vinnie?" Her smile faded and was replaced with a vexing frown. "I asked before, but I have to ask again. What happens when I disappear? Where will I go? Vinnie, I'm scared."

"I don't know," I confessed. "I don't know at all. You're the only one who's ever even asked. Maybe it's like my mom said. Maybe you'll...." I paused for a second. "Probably you'll go to a much better place. I'm sure you'll be going to a better place," I lied.

"Okay," she said, a half grin forming on her face. "Okay, that doesn't sound so bad."

"Wait! I must ask you something, you must tell me! Don't fade before I have a chance to ask...." Before I could finish my sentence, Raquel had faded away. I fell to my hands and knees. "Was it all an act?"

After a long session of heavy breathing and sorrow, I was able to drag myself onto one of the chairs. I sat there for a long while, elbows on my knees, facing downwards. I didn't know whether to laugh, to cry, or to rage at the heavens, so instead I opted to just sit there feeling sorry for myself.

How much time had passed, I had no idea. It seemed like hours, but it was probably only minutes. I didn't know what to do from there. For a while I contemplated simply sitting on that chair for the rest of my life.

"Why? Why? Why?" A familiar phrase woke me from my trance. My head snapped up as I looked around. It took a second, but my brain soon realized it was a male voice. I turned my head to the right and then back to the left, where I was greeted by a familiar looking ghost.

"Franklyn?" I asked.

"Yes! Franklyn Murphy!" the ghost excitedly said. "But how did you...?"

I cut him off. "Long story. It was Raquel Cobb, she killed you. She lured you out here in an effort to seduce you, but wound up killing you instead."

"Oh, okay," said the confused apparition.

"Is that all you wanted? Because you really should be fading away right now, and that doesn't look to be the case."

"Um, I don't know anything about that. I did want to ask you a favor, though."

I sighed. "Sure, why not? What is it?"

"I wanted to propose to my girlfriend Maria—you know, before I was killed. I want her to get my engagement ring as a sign that I truly loved her."

"An engagement ring? I suppose that's one way of getting over your commitment issues. I'm not sure that's what Elizabeth meant, though, when she talked to you about it."

"You know Elizabeth?"

"And Maria too. Like I said, Franklyn, long story—I really don't want to get into it right now. God, an engagement ring. Of course. Another one like that. You ghosts don't realize how cliché the whole ring to my fiancée bit is. I get visited by that type of ghost every week, it seems."

"Sorry. I don't really understand anything you're saying right now."

"Of course you don't. Is the ring in your pants pocket?" I asked, as I sat up and walked towards his body.

"I think so. I don't quite remember." I felt the pockets of the corpse carefully, and felt what seemed to be a ring

173

box. It was in his left pocket of his blue jeans. "There it is," I confirmed, as I reached in carefully and pulled the ring out.

"Yes! That's it! We need to give it to her!"

"Listen," I explained. "It's been a long day, and it's about to get longer for me. I have to make a call to the police and let them know what happened here. They are probably going to keep me here overnight to ask me questions as they do an investigation, and then I'm going to have to visit Raquel's parents, your girlfriend Maria, and your sister Elizabeth to let them know what happened. God, I'm not looking forward to those conversations. I'm telling you all of this to let you know that I just want you to sit here and shut up for right now. I'm not in the mood to answer any questions or anything like that. Please just sit here and be quiet. I'm going to pocket the ring for now…. Wait, let me just check something. Awesome, there's an inscription on the ring. 'To my beloved Maria. Love always, Franklyn.' Perfect, now she'll know the ring was intended for her and not Raquel. Okay, so what I'm going to tell Maria is that I pocketed the ring so the police couldn't keep it in their evidence locker. I'll tell her that I found it in your outstretched hand, so she thinks your last thoughts were of you trying to give her the ring, not trying to survive. Not that I blame you for trying to survive, but it's much more romantic if I tell her my lie instead."

"I guess that makes sense."

174

"Great! Anyway, I'm going to make a series of phone calls now. After the police are done here, I'll signal you and you can follow me to Maria's, okay?"

"I guess I can do that."

"Wonderful. Just sit there in the corner then, okay? Until I'm done here."

"All right." I nodded at the ghost in mock appreciation.

I called the police and let them know what I had discovered. Of course, it was a bit of an ordeal. The Evergreen police were the first to arrive on the scene, naturally, and they were initially suspicious of me, as they wondered why I was there in the first place. Handing them my private investigator license assuaged their suspicions quite a bit, and a quick phone call to Elizabeth confirming that she had sent me up there helped dispel almost all mistrust the officers initially had of me. Elizabeth was a bit irritated that neither I nor the police would go into specifics, but her night would be ruined by me soon enough.

It took a bit of work to get in contact with the Tacoma police, specifically one Officer Kelly Martinez. Eventually, though, we did get in contact with him, and he said he'd be over there as soon as possible. He also told me that I needed to stay put, as if I was planning on going anywhere, especially with the Evergreen officers staring right at me.

A thorough investigation took place. The officers grilled me pretty hard and long into the night, but ultimately were satisfied that I was merely an investigator and had nothing to do with the killings. In fact, the officers eventually came to the same conclusion as I did, that Raquel had murdered Franklyn, and that he had likely killed her either accidentally or through self-defense. The officers never admitted this, but they used a lot of my evidence to solve this case. They learned a lot of what was going on by interrogating me, but when I looked at the online reports over the following few days, they seemed to have told reporters that I had merely discovered the scene. The officers had neglected telling the reporters how exactly they solved the crime.

By the time the officers let me go and I got back home to Tacoma, it was already early in the morning. Franklyn's ghost had dutifully followed me back from Evergreen, floating the entire time next to the car as opposed to sitting next to me, the two of us not exchanging a single word the entire trip.

I had actually been up for almost twenty-four hours when I knocked on the Cobb's door to deliver the bad news. To say they were devastated would be an understatement. They had lost their only child. I didn't tell them all of the details, only that they needed to call the police to find out more. I told them to call me if they ever needed anything. I meant it too. I doubted they ever would, though.

Elizabeth was still with Maria when I arrived at Maria's duplex, Franklyn's ghost with me in tow. The news hit Maria like a ton of bricks. Elizabeth was clearly rattled as well, but she was a much stronger woman than Maria, emotionally at least, so she was able to regain her composure relatively quickly, perhaps out of necessity more than anything else.

Elizabeth pulled me aside so she could say something to me without Maria noticing. Frankly, it probably would not have mattered if she had said it right in front of her. Elizabeth told me she was relieved that her brother was not the creepy, obsessive psychopath that she had feared him to be. At the same time, though, she told me she almost wished he was if it meant he would still be alive.

Maria just sat there staring blankly. Nothing I said to her seemed to penetrate. Franklyn's spirit floated next to the poor girl, which reminded me of the ring sitting in my pocket. I pulled it out and told her that I had found the ring Franklyn had wanted to give to her. I explained that I took it from the police because I thought she would have wanted it, and it would have been a shame to have it rot in some evidence locker.

I told her that it appeared that he was going to propose to her after his hunting trip, and when he thought it was her in the cabin he was planning on proposing to her there instead. Even after he was shot, I told her that his only thought was of her, as I had found the ring in his outstretched hand as he crawled towards the door. Maria simply lost it at that point—tears flowed like a waterfall down her cheeks, and she started bawling uncontrollably.

177

I saw Franklyn come up to the girl and try to hug her in vain as he gradually faded into the ether.

Elizabeth tried to comfort her as best she could. I tried to assist, but soon realized I was more a hindrance than a help. As I left, Elizabeth thanked me as well as she could, and the two of us exchanged an awkward goodbye. I hope the two of them are all right.

I made one more stop before I went home — at my mother's house, so that I could let her know that I was okay and what had happened. To say my mother was disappointed that Raquel had ultimately turned out to be a murderer would be like saying the Grand Canyon was a small hole. Initially she was incredulous, but as soon as news reports began to appear online confirming what I had said, she realized I was telling the truth. After the initial shock had worn off, she apologized to me and then mentioned how proud she was of me for solving another mystery, and dismissed any notion I had that the whole endeavor had been a waste of time.

Where ghosts fade away to I still don't know. During the visit, I tried talking to my mom about it again. She told me that she had thought about it after Raquel asked her that question, but she had come to the conclusion that if philosophers, theologians, and scholars alike had been debating that question for years and had not come up with a definitive answer, then the question was simply too great for people like us. A copout, sure, but it was as good an answer as any, I suppose. I guess we'll all find the answer to that question someday.

At the end of the day, what did I really accomplish? I found a couple of dead bodies for the police to investigate, sure, but otherwise, who benefited from all of this? Maybe finding the bodies would bring some peace and comfort to the families, eventually. I can only hope.

It seemed like the news devastated them, though. The Cobbs certainly didn't seem to find peace and comfort finding out about the death of their daughter and her apparent mental illness. Maria certainly didn't seem to find peace and comfort finding out about her best friend's betrayal and the death of her boyfriend. Even knowing her boyfriend loved her deeply and wanted to get married seemed to only make his death more heartbreaking for her. Elizabeth certainly didn't seem to find peace and comfort, unless finding out that her brother wasn't a creepy, obsessive stalker counted. I suppose that one could go either way.

For me, the whole effort had been for naught. I certainly didn't benefit from all of this. I didn't gain any fame or fortune. I didn't gain true love. I'm not sure that I even really helped anybody except for a couple of ghosts, and at least with one of the two it is highly debatable. I didn't even get a thank you. Not even from Raquel, even though she promised. So like I said, ghosts are assholes.

EPILOGUE

I woke up in the early afternoon the next day. I didn't get much sleep for obvious reasons, and was still in a foul mood. Still in my pajamas, I tried to calm myself by playing a game of solitaire, but quickly realized that anger and hunger prevented me from concentrating on the game. I decided to go outside and get some fresh air.

I skipped the shower altogether, put on some sweats I had lying around, and after picking up my keys, wallet, and cell phone I began walking towards my local eatery to get myself an unhealthy lunch. I was completely demoralized. As I walked, head down, hands in my pocket, I heard a man's voice from behind me.

"Excuse me?" he said.

"Yes, what is it?" I growled, turning around, suddenly realizing I was talking to a ghost. He was a stocky ghost of relatively normal height with a big beard, wearing a Dodgers shirt, a Dodgers hat, and a pair of blue jeans. I was fumbling around for my Bluetooth headset when

I realized I had forgotten to bring it with me. I sighed heavily, but continued to converse with the man. In my current mood, I simply did not care if people thought I was crazy.

"I'm sorry to bother you," he said. "I was just wondering. Do you know who won the World Series?"

"The Houston Astros!" I yelled, eliciting a few silent stares from bystanders.

"The Houston Astros? Really?"

"Yes, really!" I screamed.

"Huh, that's too bad, I was a big Dodgers fan. Oh well, congratulations to them, I suppose. Thank you very much for letting me know."

"You're welcome," I snapped back as I saw the man disappear before my very eyes. I walked a few steps before I had a sudden realization of what had happened. My mood lightened as I stopped, looked back over my shoulder, and simply said to myself, "Imagine that."

About the Author

James Kirst lives in the Evergreen State in a humble little abode within the forested city of Dupont. There, he earned his Master's Degree at the University of Washington. Commuting up north to Tacoma, he has worked as a senior programmer and software development lead for almost ten years.

With a borderline obsessive interest in the paranormal, James has conducted intensive study into the subject. To that end, he has visited some of the most haunted places in the United States including Salem, the LaLaurie Mansion of New Orleans, and his personal favorite, the Shanghai Tunnels of Portland, Oregon.

As an avid fan of mystery both in fiction and in real life,

he has done extensive research into police procedurals, the machinations of detective work, and life as a private investigator.

A big sports fan, James is sure to either be watching or participating in one when not writing about or educating himself in one of the aforementioned subjects. In fact, he has won multiple championships in bowling and slow pitch softball and has made several appearances as a softball All-Star where he was given the privilege of playing in Cheney Stadium. He is still seeking that elusive kickball title, however.

www.ingramcontent.com/pod-product-compliance
Lightning Source LLC
Chambersburg PA
CBHW022116170626
46808CB00002B/747